D1079793

000003000749

SPECIAL MESSAGE TO READERS

THE ULVERSCROFT FOUNDATION
(registered UK charity number 264873)
was established in 1972 to provide funds for research, diagnosis and treatment of eye diseases.
Examples of major projects funded by the Ulverscroft Foundation are:-

- The Children's Eye Unit at Moorfields Eye Hospital, London
- The Ulverscroft Children's Eye Unit at Great Ormond Street Hospital for Sick Children
- Funding research into eye diseases and treatment at the Department of Ophthalmology, University of Leicester
- The Ulverscroft Vision Research Group, Institute of Child Health
- Twin operating theatres at the Western Ophthalmic Hospital, London
- The Chair of Ophthalmology at the Royal Australian College of Ophthalmologists

You can help further the work of the Foundation by making a donation or leaving a legacy. Every contribution is gratefully received. If you would like to help support the Foundation or require further information, please contact:

THE ULVERSCROFT FOUNDATION
The Green, Bradgate Road, Anstey
Leicester LE7 7FU, England
Tel: (0116) 236 4325

website: www.foundation.ulverscroft.com

THE RANSOM

Eve Masters's life is thrown into chaos when her beloved David is kidnapped on their home island of Crete. Determined to track down those involved, Eve finds herself at odds with the police and suspecting her own friends. Then David escapes; but, ill and unable to remember who his kidnappers were, he is rushed to hospital — where someone tries to silence him for good. Can Eve get to the bottom of the mystery before the kidnappers turn their sights on her?

Books by Irena Nieslony
in the Linford Romance Library:

DANGEROUS AFFAIR
DEAD IN THE WATER
DEATHLY CHRISTMAS
AFRICAN ADVENTURE
THE LOST YEARS

IRENA NIESLONY

THE RANSOM

Complete and Unabridged

LINFORD
Leicester

First published in Great Britain in 2015

First Linford Edition
published 2019

A catalogue record for this book is available from the British Library.

ISBN 978–1–4448–4260–9

Published by
F. A. Thorpe (Publishing)
Anstey, Leicestershire

Set by Words & Graphics Ltd.
Anstey, Leicestershire
Printed and bound in Great Britain by
T. J. International Ltd., Padstow, Cornwall

This book is printed on acid-free paper

1

In the corner of a basement, David Baker sat hunched up on a mattress which was on the floor. He had been blindfolded for the journey there, so he had no idea whose basement it was or which village he was in. Now, although the blindfold had been taken off, his hands and feet were tied and he had a gag in his mouth.

David hadn't put his watch on that morning so he wasn't sure how long he had been there, but his kidnapper had come down once to give him food and to let him use the bathroom. He was relieved that there was a toilet in the basement as he had an awful feeling that he might be there for some time.

When his kidnapper had visited him, he had untied David and taken the gag out, but had kept his gun pointing at him the whole time. As David was worried that there could be another person upstairs, he hadn't dared make a break for it; not yet at least.

He had been taken from his home by two people, not just one, and thought it possible that the other kidnapper was waiting upstairs. No, it probably wasn't safe to try and escape.

Now, for the second time he heard steps coming downstairs, and a moment later a plate of food was put in front of him. The brown slush on the plate looked revolting, but he knew he had to keep his strength up.

'What do you want with me? Why have you done this?' David asked his kidnapper.

'You'll find out soon enough,' was the reply. 'Now eat.'

David ate what he could bear before being tied up again. The kidnapper had a mask on, but David thought his voice sounded familiar. However, he couldn't quite pinpoint it and it was driving him crazy. He was also sure that the other kidnapper was a woman, but he had only had a glimpse of her and she too had been wearing a mask.

Is this it? he thought miserably after the kidnapper had left. *My life has got so much better in the past year, but now I might not even have the chance to marry Eve. There's got to be some way of getting out of here . . .*

* * *

Eve Masters sat on her couch with her friend Annie Davies, sipping a cup of hot, sweet tea. Her eyes were red from crying and for once she didn't care what her make-up looked like.

'Annie,' Eve sobbed, 'they're going to kill David, aren't they?'

'Of course not,' Annie replied, giving her friend a hug. 'Look at the letter again. They just want money. He's worth more alive than dead.'

Eve burst into floods of tears again.

'They want 100,000 Euros by Friday,' she muttered in between her tears. 'It's Wednesday today. Yes, I'm rich, but my money isn't all in cash. I have stocks and shares and other investments. I can't get that much money together so quickly.'

'I'm sure they'll give you a bit longer if you explain the situation,' Annie replied, trying to sound optimistic even though she was far from it. 'Perhaps you should involve the police.'

'No, I can't do that,' Eve said firmly, having finally stopped crying. 'They said no police, otherwise David dies. Oh, Annie, I think it would be better if I started to look for him myself.'

'Kidnappers always say no police, Eve. Anyway, you have absolutely no idea where David is. You wouldn't even know where to start looking. I don't think you've got a choice.'

Eve nodded; she knew Annie was right. She was out of her depth this time and she probably had no option but to tell the police.

Please God, let David be alright, Eve prayed quietly to herself while Annie went to get her another cup of tea.

This was so hard to believe. A couple of days ago everything was fine. Eve, returning from a trip to England, was so excited about seeing David again. Now everything was a complete mess.

Eve took another tissue out of her bag and wiped her face. She looked in her mirror and was shocked at what she saw.

'I'd better put on some make-up before we go to the police station,' she said to Annie who had just come back into the room. 'I can't go out looking like this.'

Annie was relieved that Eve was starting to sound like her normal self. Even though she was a naturally attractive woman, Eve wouldn't leave home without doing her make-up and styling her hair, not even to walk her dog, Portia.

However, Eve suddenly had another thought.

'What if I'm being watched? The kidnappers could follow us and see we're going to the police station. And if we ask the police to come here, it wouldn't be any better either, would it?'

'You're right, Eve. Perhaps you'd better just phone the police.'

Eve nodded, suddenly feeling more like herself again now that it had been decided what the first step should be.

Whoever's got David had better watch out, she thought to herself. *I'm going to pull myself together and get David back, preferably without giving them any money.*

Eve steeled herself to ring the police. She knew that Detective Chief Inspector Dimitris Kastrinakis wouldn't be happy to hear from her again so soon. He had been the detective in charge of the recent murder cases which Eve had got involved in. He didn't appreciate her amateur sleuthing. The last one had only been a couple of months previously.

'Detective Chief Inspector Kastrinakis has always told me off for poking my nose in police business,' Eve said to Annie. 'However, this is completely different. If he doesn't come forward with a plan quickly, I will interfere, mark my words. After all, David's life is at stake and I may have to be the one who rescues him.'

Annie just stared at her friend, realising that Eve would go to any lengths to save David. There was one thing Annie was certain about and that was how much Eve loved him.

2

It was only a couple of days previously that Eve Masters was sitting on a plane on the short flight from Athens to Chania which was on the island of Crete in Greece. She had caught this flight a couple of hours after the longer journey from London Heathrow to Athens.

Eve gazed dreamily at her engagement ring. It was beautiful; one large diamond surrounded by seven smaller ones, set in a platinum band. She couldn't believe how lucky she was to be engaged to the handsome and compassionate David Baker.

Sipping her complimentary coffee, Eve reminisced about David's proposal. It was one of her favourite pastimes and she would often find herself reliving that afternoon. It still made her tingle, although whether it would still do so if she knew the truth about it, is another matter.

You see, David was in fact going to ask Eve to live with him, not get married. Yes, he wanted her to be his wife more than anything, but he saw her as an independent and modern woman and not the type of person who would ever want to get married. He felt that if he asked her to be his wife, it might frighten her away and he would lose her forever. However, he hesitated when he was about to ask her to move in with him. He was even a little nervous to ask her this, and while he paused, Eve jumped in.

She was under the impression that he was going to propose marriage and immediately said she would be delighted to be his wife. Although David was stunned, he didn't bother to correct her mistake as marriage was what he wanted as well. She fell into his arms and they kissed passionately, Eve completely unaware of the misunderstanding that had occurred.

Looking out of the plane window, Eve thought what a pity it was that the wedding had to be the following June; she would have liked to have married straight away but her dream wedding would take time to organise.

David had been both shocked and surprised when she had told him that she wanted to get married on a beach with all her friends from England attending, followed by a reception at one of the five star hotels. He was expecting to have an intimate service at a registry office, but he saw her face fall when he suggested it.

'But David, you've been married before,' Eve had said. 'I haven't and I would like all my friends to come to the wedding, plus I want a beautiful white dress, a big reception, bridesmaids, the whole works.'

David had looked at Eve's mournful face and he began to soften. Although she didn't actually have that many true friends — most of the people she knew in England being acquaintances and ex-business colleagues — he knew that she wanted to show him off and who was he to deny her that pleasure for one day. In the end he capitulated.

Eve had taken over the arrangements for the wedding. David was happy about this as she was so much better than he was at organising things. She had contacted a wedding planning company who were more than happy to help arrange Eve and David's wedding, especially when she mentioned that there could be as many as one hundred and twenty guests.

Thinking about how long it was until their big day, Eve's smile suddenly turned into a frown. *What am I going to do until then?* she thought.

David indeed was a little anxious about Eve's boredom threshold. Cretan life suited him very well. Previously an actor, he was now a novelist and he loved the peace and tranquillity of the island. Eve however, had been a showbiz agent back in England and she loved the buzz of London. It hadn't taken her long to become bored on Crete.

Eve had moved to the island just over a year previously and since then there had been a series of murders in and around the village she lived in. Each time Eve had decided to do a bit of private sleuthing herself which she had found very exciting. Although she had a knack for detective work, she had put her life in danger time and time again. She had a tendency to act recklessly which worried David immensely, as did her ability to get over these incidents easily. He feared that she would continually rush into the next dangerous situation without thinking about it and one day, God forbid, could end up dead.

The flight attendant came round to clear the coffee cups away and Eve realised that it wasn't long before the plane would land in Chania. Even so, she closed her eyes so that she could imagine her reunion with David. She couldn't wait to see him and pictured his striking face. He often looked serious, but she knew he would melt as soon as he saw her. He always did and his face lit up as if he were a different person.

A few moments later the pilot announced that they were about to land at Chania airport. Eve opened her eyes immediately and smiled. She had missed David very much on this trip. In fact, each time she went away, she found she missed David more and more. Perhaps holidays without him would become a thing of the past.

* * *

As Eve got off the plane, she smiled again. It was hot and sunny, just as she liked the weather to be. In fact, if England had Crete's wonderful climate Eve would never have left.

Eve was excited. After nine days apart, she was about to see David and she couldn't wait. Once again, she closed her eyes and pictured him with his jet black hair and piercing blue eyes. He was absolutely gorgeous and she wondered why there hadn't been that many women in his life. She guessed that he must be very particular where women were concerned and it made her feel special that he had chosen her to be his wife. He had been married once before, but that had been when he was very young and it hadn't lasted long.

Within minutes Eve was in baggage reclaim, but a quarter of an hour later, she started to get impatient when there was no sign of any luggage.

Really, she thought, *they're quicker at Heathrow and it's a far larger airport than here*.

Eve tried to pass the time by looking at the people standing around the carousel, deciding who were tourists and who were ex-pats. In the end she decided most people were on holiday; they definitely looked as if they could do with a week or two in the sun.

Eve's eyes moved around the rest of

baggage reclaim. She was always curious and interested in everything that went on. Unfortunately, some people would call her just plain nosey, but she did have a general interest in human nature. Eve looked at the other carousel and then saw somebody she recognised. She had to look twice as she couldn't believe her eyes.

My goodness, it was Joanna Neonakis. What on earth was she doing back here? Eve had almost forgotten about her.

Memories of the murders which had taken place the previous June came rushing back. With her engagement and the preparations for the wedding taking up Eve's time in-between then and now, it seemed like a lifetime ago.

Eve had found the first murder victim back then, a woman called Lucy Fowler. The murderer had turned out to be Lucy's brother-in-law, Paul Fowler, with whom she had had an affair some time previously. Still in love with Lucy and finding out that she was having an affair with the local stud, Yiannis Neonakis, Paul had killed them both.

Nobody knew that Yiannis had got married in England earlier in the year, but his wife, Joanna, turned up at Yiannis's funeral and stayed for a week to sort out legalities.

On the day of the funeral, Eve had been excited about finding out more about Joanna, but that was the day David and Eve decided to get married and she was thrown into a whirlwind of emotions. By the time she had come back down to earth, Joanna had left the island.

Since then, Eve had thought about Joanna occasionally and it had even briefly crossed her mind that she was the mastermind behind another of the murders, one which had taken place the previous December.

A virtual newcomer to the island, Jennifer Anderson, had been murdered by her nephew, James, on Christmas Eve, but he was later found dead in an

Athens' hotel room. His killer had never been found. Eve became convinced it was Yiannis's widow, Joanna.

Seeing Joanna again brought everything back and she became quite excited, although she knew she shouldn't be.

She'd promised David she wouldn't interfere in anything dangerous again, but this was almost too interesting to let go of.

There was something strange and not quite right about that woman. For a start, how did she get Yiannis to marry her in a matter of a couple of weeks? Then she came over for her husband's funeral, but only stayed a short time and only put one of his houses on the market, keeping the other house.

Eve started to feel guilty. She had been so careful these last few months just spending her free time arranging the wedding, but with the wedding company's assistance, a lot of the preparations had been taken care of. What was she to do now? This was one mystery she would love to solve.

Eve glanced at Joanna only to find her staring at her. For a moment their eyes met, but then Joanna looked away.

Well, really, thought Eve. *How rude. I'm certain she knows who I am*.

As Joanna went to pick up her very large suitcase from the carousel, three men rushed to help her. Eve felt the green-eyed monster take over. Was that woman more attractive than she was? Eve couldn't see it and couldn't believe that Joanna had so many men fawning all over her.

Joanna Neonakis was indeed a beautiful woman. Like Eve, she was slim, but that's where the similarities ended. While Eve was petite, Joanna was at least five feet ten, to which she added a few more inches with her stiletto heels.

How can she fly in those shoes? Eve thought. *They must be so uncomfortable*.

Joanna had long silky brown hair. Eve remembered her tossing her hair back in The Black Cat pub that last time they'd met on the island, just like in one of those ads for a television hair commercial. Some of the men in the bar had been frozen to their seats and just stared at her, open mouthed.

She also had the advantage of only being in her early thirties, about ten years younger than Eve. Eve suddenly felt old and drab and certainly didn't feel as stunning as she was. Although Eve was vain, she was the first to find fault with herself.

Come on Eve, pull yourself together, she told herself. *You're being ridiculous and insecure. You're going to marry the most wonderful man in the world so you have nothing to worry about.*

Eve was, of course, a very attractive woman as well. She had shoulder length blonde hair, striking emerald green eyes and was naturally slim.

However, when Joanna walked by with some stranger helping her with all her luggage, Eve fumed, especially as a few moments later she attempted to drag her suitcase off the carousel on her own.

⋆ ⋆ ⋆

As Eve left baggage reclaim, she saw David waiting for her. However, he hadn't seen her, so Eve stopped for a moment just to admire him from a distance. He looked so gorgeous that she felt her heart beating faster and she had a tingling feeling in her stomach. Then all of a sudden, that awful woman stopped to talk to him.

How dare she? How dare Joanna talk to my fiancé? Eve fumed.

Eve stormed over to David who didn't see her until she was standing right next to him. As David started to smile, Eve flung her arms around him.

'Darling, I've missed you so much. It's good to be home.'

Then she kissed him. Strangely enough, David seemed a little embarrassed. He never usually minded public shows of affection if they'd been apart for so long. Unfortunately, Eve noticed and wasn't happy about his attitude.

David was indeed a little uncomfortable, but not because he cared at all for Joanna, but because someone was so obviously watching them. However, he was also secretly pleased that Eve seemed so happy to be back on Crete. He had been worried that she would become homesick for England during her trip, but it didn't seem as if she had and he was relieved.

'You remember my fiancée, Eve Masters,' David asked Joanna.

'Oh . . . yes,' she said, more or less dismissing his remark.

'You're Joanna Neonakis, aren't you?' Eve asked, trying to be pleasant and not show her true feelings. 'Well, I'm surprised to see you back here.'

'I'm here for a month or so, sorting out the paperwork on my husband's estate. Greek bureaucracy does seem to be very complicated. I hardly got anything sorted out when I was here in June.'

'I'm not surprised. Everything is complicated here,' David replied.

'Well, we must be on our way, mustn't we, darling,' Eve said, putting her hand ever so gently on David's arm as if to make a point.

'I'm sure I'll see you around,' Joanna said, looking pointedly at David.

'Yes, I expect so,' David replied, picking up Eve's cases.

Once out of Joanna's earshot, David turned to face Eve.

'Well, well, Eve, what was all that about? You aren't jealous of Joanna, are you?'

He had suddenly realised near the end of the conversation that Joanna was possibly flirting with him and now it suddenly clicked that Eve might, after all, be resentful that Joanna was paying him so much attention. He had no idea why. Didn't Eve realise that the only woman he wanted was her?

'Me, jealous of Joanna? Why should I be?' she asked with a tinge of annoyance in her voice.

'Well,' David remarked, 'she did seem to be flirting with me and I know you hate it when other women make a move towards me.'

'Humph,' Eve retorted. 'There was a time when you never noticed that women were flirting with you. I'm sure it's me who's made you aware that many women do find you attractive. I wish I'd never said anything.'

Even though she had an exuberant and extrovert personality, Eve had always been insecure in personal relationships and this one was no exception.

'Eve, darling, don't doubt yourself so much. After all, I did ask you to marry me.'

'No you didn't, David,' Eve admitted for the first time. She had realised a couple of weeks previously that he hadn't actually asked her, but she had put it out of her mind, pretending it didn't happen as it did.

'In a roundabout way I asked you,' Eve conceded. 'When I interrupted you, you could have been planning to ask me something completely different.'

Eve had never thought he was going to do anything but propose marriage, but now her insecurity was finally getting the better of her.

'Of course I wasn't going to ask you anything else,' David lied, feeling it best to hide the truth from Eve.

If he told her he was just going to ask her to live with him, it might make her even more insecure than she was already.

'Now, come on, Eve, let's go home. You have a busy few days coming up.'

Eve nodded, feeling a little happier. She knew she was being silly, but she did feel her relationship with David did balance on a precipice. She had frightened him so much searching for murderers that she was surprised that he was still with her. However, she needed excitement in her life and could never be a stay-at-home wife . . .

3

The following day, Eve had arranged to take her friend, Jane Phillips, into Chania, which was their nearest major town, to look for a maid-of-honour dress for her.

Jane was moving back to England in a few days' time after having lived on Crete since the previous December. Eve thought she would be desperate to go back after all she had been through, but Jane was sad to be leaving. She had managed to cope with her experiences surprisingly well for such a shy and nervous young woman.

Jane's father, John Phillips, who had lived alone on Crete, had been killed the previous summer and when Jane came over to sort out his property, she fell in love with James Anderson who ended up killing his aunt. Then poor Jane had the misfortune to go out with

Paul Fowler who also turned out to be a killer, murdering both his sister-in-law and her lover, Yiannis Neonakis. Eve wondered if she could have remained as calm as Jane after such experiences.

After their shopping expedition, Eve and Jane decided to go to The Black Cat, the local English bar run by Ken and Jan Stewart, a couple in their mid thirties who had moved from London about five years previously.

As they entered the bar, Eve stopped dead in her tracks.

'What is it Eve?' Jane asked.

'It's Kevin Fowler. He's with Joanna Neonakis again,' she whispered.

Kevin Fowler, Lucy's husband, had met Joanna on the day of Yiannis's funeral and they had spent a great deal of time together during the week she was on Crete.

'I know his marriage was finished long before Paul killed Lucy,' Eve continued, 'but Joanna and Yiannis had only recently got married. Or do you think she married him for the money?'

'Hasn't she got her own business, Eve?'

'Yes, but it doesn't mean it's successful.'

'Is Kevin that well off?'

'I have no idea,' Eve replied. 'But I don't think he's short of a bob or two.'

Joanna suddenly glanced at them and Eve felt conspicuous so she headed straight for a table.

'We'll sit here,' she told Jane. 'What would you like to drink? I fancy a nice cold gin and tonic.'

Eve had dropped her car off at home and they had walked to the bar. She felt there was nothing like relaxing with a cold G and T after a busy morning shopping. And it had been busy. Eve had been determined to find the perfect dress for Jane which surprised Jane immensely. She knew Eve would want to be the centre of attention on her big day, so why was Eve trying so hard to make Jane look stunning?

Eve had, in fact, shocked herself. Despite being quite a self-centred person, Eve felt a great deal of sympathy for Jane. Her friend had been through so much in the past year, but despite being a shy and anxious girl, she had come through all her problems without breaking down. She thought Jane should also enjoy her wedding day and she wanted to make it a day for her to remember. In addition, Eve had single male friends coming and perhaps one of them might be attracted to her. As far as she knew, none of them were murderers!

As soon as they had got their drinks, Eve spoke.

'I am going to miss you, Jane.'

'I'll miss you too,' Jane replied. 'But I need to work again, not only financially, but because I want to; very much. I am starting to get bored.'

Eve nodded sympathetically, thinking of her days as a showbiz agent. In a way, she wished she hadn't given it up; the job was in her blood, but then she wouldn't have met David. Why couldn't she have both? However, she knew that

David would never move back to England.

Eve stole another look at Joanna and Kevin. They were laughing and Eve wished they were sitting nearer so she might be able to hear what they were saying.

'You keep looking at Joanna and Kevin,' Jane said. 'Do you think they're having an affair?'

'God, no,' Eve exclaimed. 'Well, I don't think their relationship has gone that far yet, but I think they might be heading that way.'

'He's so much older than she is.'

'Yes, he is. Perhaps she's a serial killer. Perhaps she marries men for their money and then kills them. First Yiannis and now Kevin.'

The thought had just struck Eve.

'But she didn't kill Yiannis, did she? Paul did.'

'Yes, you're right about that, but it could be because he got in first. I mean, she didn't seem upset on the day of her husband's funeral at all and she was quite flirtatious with Kevin when they came in here.'

Jane agreed, but inside she was thinking that Eve's mind was working overtime.

Eve, on the other hand, was thinking something completely different.

I won't tell Jane that I have suspicions that Joanna might be the mastermind behind the murder of James Anderson. I don't want to remind her about him.

'Eve, you seem miles away. Are you alright?'

'Yes, I'm fine. I was just thinking what a strange year it's been — since I moved over to Crete I mean. I certainly wouldn't have expected to be involved in so many murder cases.'

'Well, I hope you're not going to get involved in finding out more about Joanna. David wouldn't be too happy.'

'Really, Jane, give me more credit,' Eve lied, feeling slightly guilty. 'Yes, she does interest me, but I wouldn't put my relationship on the line for her, especially as she has already been flirting with David.'

'Has she really?' Jane replied. 'Well, what an awful woman.'

'Yes, she is. I think she wants to rile me.'

'Why on earth would she want to do that?'

'I have absolutely no idea. She's obviously taken a dislike to me. Well, the feeling's mutual.'

As they were talking, Kevin and Joanna got up to leave and both Jane and Eve noticed they were holding hands.

'I wonder what Wayne thinks of all this?' Eve asked. 'Both he and Justin weren't happy that their dad was hanging around with Joanna.'

Kevin's younger son, Justin, had arrived on Crete the day after his mother was killed and Wayne a couple of days later. Kevin eventually discovered that Wayne had lost his job back in England and it was decided that he would try to keep his uncle Paul's gardening and maintenance business going. If it worked out, he would bring his wife and three children over to live on Crete.

Eve had to admit that she didn't see Wayne hanging around much with his father, so perhaps there was a rift between them. Sometimes Wayne would join her and David in The Black Cat for a drink. He seemed to be settling in to life on Crete and the business was doing relatively well so far. Eve had employed him as her gardener now that Paul had been locked up.

'How's Justin by the way?' Jane asked.

Justin was bi-polar, but was doing well on his medication. He and David's niece, Emma, who came to Crete during the summer to work in a bar, had become quite an item.

'Oh, Justin and Emma are still seeing each other. It seems pretty serious, even though they are only in their early twenties. They've both got a year left at university so anything could happen.'

Jane nodded in agreement.

'I'm a bit hungry now,' Eve said. 'Do you want anything to eat, Jane?'

'I wouldn't mind a toasted sandwich.'

'What a good idea. Think I'll have cheese and tomato in mine.' Eve was a vegetarian and had been so for twenty years.

She went up to the bar to order the food.

'You don't look too happy, Ken. Is everything alright?' Eve asked when she reached the bar.

'Well, not really. We've got some hefty bills, including one from the tax office. Everything has gone up. All these austerity measures are not making it easy to run a business over here.'

'You don't think you're going to have to pack up and go home, do you?'

'We wanted to stay here forever, but now our future is very uncertain. We don't want to go, but we may have to, that is if we can sell the bar and our property. I hear it's difficult with so many people selling up.'

'You've done such a good job with the bar, Ken. It would be very sad if you had to leave.'

'Thanks Eve. We're not giving up yet . . . I'll give your food order to Jan.'

Eve went back to her table thinking how awful it was that things kept changing. Ken and Jan were good hosts; one or other of them was always there for breakfasts from ten o'clock onwards and they stayed open all day until the early hours. It was nice to have a place where the English could congregate and discuss things, though there were certain members of the English community Eve would rather not see on a regular basis. As if reading her thoughts, her arch enemy, Betty Jones, walked into The Black Cat with her husband, Don.

From the moment they had met, Betty and Eve had taken an instant dislike to each other. Betty liked to think she was in charge of organising events for the English community and was a bossy and antagonistic woman. She felt that Eve was trying to usurp her position which was nonsense of course.

Eve, who had come from the world of show business, had no interest in taking over and organising a group of ex-pats. Betty also thought Eve wasn't good enough for David, but by criticising her in front of him, she had managed to alienate him. Betty had become quite upset to lose David as a friend and stupidly blamed Eve.

When Betty entered the bar, she ignored Eve completely and went to sit down, while Don went up to order drinks. On his way back to his table, he stopped to talk to Eve.

'Hello Eve, how are you?' he asked

'I'm fine, thanks. I've just got back from a trip to England.'

'I expect you enjoyed yourself.'

'Yes, it was lovely to see friends and to go to the theatre again. How are you?'

It had become common knowledge

that Don and Betty's marriage was going through a bad patch. Whenever they were together, they either argued or ignored each other. As Jane had gone to the ladies, he decided to confide in Eve.

'Surviving, Eve,' Don replied. 'All I can say is that I'm looking forward to the drama group starting again. Betty says she's not going to go, thank goodness. I'm so pleased you've decided to keep running it.'

'I'm sorry things aren't going well between you and Betty,' Eve remarked, not caring if she was being too personal. 'Have you ever thought of leaving her?'

Don was a little shocked at Eve's forthright question, but then they had talked bluntly many times and had become good friends.

'I have thought about it, but financially, I can't see it working. Our house isn't that big so if we sold it and shared the profits, we probably wouldn't have enough to buy a smaller property each. We haven't much in the way of savings and live on our pensions.'

'I'm sorry,' Eve said. 'It must be difficult living like you do.'

Don nodded and then Eve noticed Betty glaring over at her.

'I think you'd better get back to your table, Don. Your wife is staring at me and her expression isn't very friendly.'

Don smiled and went back to join Betty just as Jane came back.

'What was all that about?' Jane asked Eve.

'Oh, it was nothing important. I believe Don and Betty's marriage is on the rocks, but Don doesn't think there's any way out.'

'Poor Don having to put up with Betty. He seems such a nice, gentle sort of man.'

'He is. I expect Betty was nicer when he first met her, but she's such an old busybody now and takes no interest in him. Mind you, I expect he's glad that she's not keen on the theatre so he can have a few nights a week away from her.'

Jane smiled, but inside thought that not many relationships ended up 'happily ever after'.

Kevin and Lucy weren't happy, nor are Don and Betty. She thought Annie and Pete were, but who knew for sure.

Eve and Jane stayed in the bar for a little while longer to eat their sandwiches and have another drink. Betty completely ignored Eve for the duration of their stay. Eve was quite annoyed as she had to admit that she enjoyed their quarrels!

Eventually Eve and Jane left; Eve looking forward to spending her evening with David. He, as usual, had been working hard on his novel since early morning.

Jane went home to carry on packing, wishing in a way that she wasn't leaving.

4

The following day, Eve slept in late. She'd had a wonderful evening with David the night before. They had gone to the Italian restaurant, Bella Sophia, in a nearby seaside resort. It was a bit more upmarket than most of the tavernas, though not quite as expensive as the Italian restaurant in Chania which was Eve's favourite place to dine. Still, she had become very fond of Bella Sophia and as she was known to tip considerably better than most people, she was always treated well, with little goodies arriving as freebies throughout the meal.

Eve and David had spent the evening mainly talking about their wedding. He was delighted that she seemed so excited about it.

She avoided mentioning Joanna and her suspicions about her and felt quite proud about her ability to be restrained. She was, in fact, desperate to talk about her thoughts and of her distrust of the woman, but she knew how irritated David would be if she did.

After having a nightcap in a local bar, David had spent the night with Eve, but he had got up early to go home to work on his novel.

'Eve darling, I've brought you a coffee,' he said before he left. 'I'll see you later.'

Eve woke up and yawned.

'Do you have to go so early, David? I presume it is early, isn't it?'

'It's seven thirty and yes, you know I work best earlier in the day.'

'I suppose so.'

Eve put her arms around David and kissed him. For a moment, he was tempted to stay, but he knew he would regret it later.

'I'll see you in the afternoon, darling. I'd better go now before you tempt me back into bed.'

'That wouldn't be so bad, would it?'

Eve grinned wickedly.

David smiled in return, blowing her a kiss as he left the room.

Eve took a sip of her coffee and then lay back down to have another five minutes sleep. However, when she woke up again, it was almost ten fifteen.

* * *

Eve sunbathed in her back garden for a couple of hours that morning, deciding to take her dog, Portia, out for a walk in the evening when it got a little cooler.

At around twelve thirty she went indoors to get a drink and noticed that there was a letter on her front door mat. She was surprised as her post went to a PO Box in the post office, but thought it was probably an invitation from one of the locals. However, when she opened it, she couldn't believe what she was reading. Was it a joke? She screwed the letter up as soon as she had read it and went to sit down on her couch, but a couple of minutes later she had to read it again. It had been typed and wasn't signed.

We *have David. If you want to see him again, it will cost you 100,000 Euros. You have until Friday to get the money. We will let you know where the meeting place will be. Don't tell the police. You will be sorry if you do.*

Trembling, Eve got up and started pacing with the letter in her hand. Who on earth had written it? Eve had absolutely no idea, but whoever had done it was definitely serious.

'This isn't happening,' Eve said out loud, starting to sob. She was usually so tough and knew exactly what to do in most situations, but nobody had ever presented her with a ransom demand before.

Joanna, Eve suddenly thought. *She's the most likely suspect, but would she have the strength to physically take on someone the size of David? She must have had a male accomplice. However, I don't know if I believe that she would have got Kevin involved. Kevin seems straight to me and he's David's friend. Perhaps she's got another partner in crime.*

Desperate to talk to someone, Eve wiped away the tears and rushed to the phone.

She quickly dialled the number, hoping her friend was at home, and sighed with relief when the phone was picked up at the other end.

'Annie, are you able to come over, please. It's urgent. I'll tell you all about it when you get here.'

Annie Davies agreed to come, but suspected that Eve was blowing whatever she wanted to tell her way out of proportion. She had got to know Eve well over the past year and knew she was prone to exaggeration and embellishment, but she still liked her very much.

Annie and her husband, Pete, had lived on Crete for a few years, having retired early, he from the police force and she from teaching. Annie and Eve had become friends almost as soon as

Eve had arrived on Crete, even though they had very different personalities. Annie hadn't led such a glamorous and exciting life as Eve had and was a little envious of her, while Eve was slightly jealous of Annie and Pete's long and happy marriage.

Eve was unable to sit still while she was waiting for Annie, yet it took less than ten minutes for her friend to arrive. When the doorbell rang, Eve rushed to answer it and started sobbing again as soon as Annie came in.

'Eve, what's wrong,' Annie asked. 'I've never seen you like this.'

She became a little nervous. Annie was used to Eve always being so sure of herself and basically not being afraid of anything, sometimes going feet first into dangerous situations.

'Oh Annie, this was pushed through my door a little while ago. What am I to do? I'll hold the letter out for you to read it in case it has fingerprints on it, but I expect that whoever wrote it was too clever and put gloves on.'

Annie read the note and then spoke more calmly than she felt.

'The first thing you're going to do, Eve, is have a hot cup of sweet tea and calm down. Then we'll go from there.'

Eve nodded, relieved that Annie was taking charge. For once in her life, she didn't want to be in control.

* * *

Feeling a little calmer after her cup of tea, Eve went and got her mobile phone. In it she had stored the number of Detective Chief Inspector Dimitris Kastrinakis.

She decided she would rather speak to him personally than dial 112, the emergency number in Greece; even though she knew that he wouldn't be too happy to hear from her yet again. At least she wouldn't be reporting a murder this time.

Eve hesitated before dialling.

'Am I really doing the right thing Annie? They told me not to ring the police. What if they've bugged my phone?'

'And how would they have done that?' Annie asked gently.

'I don't know; it was just a thought.'

'I doubt if your phone's been bugged,' Annie continued. 'You carry your mobile with you at all times. However, if it makes you feel better, you can use mine.'

'Thanks. You're right. I'm not thinking straight at all, am I?'

Despite Eve knowing she was being over zealous, she still took Annie's mobile and put in the inspector's number. However, she still hesitated in pressing the call button.

What will he be able to do? If he starts questioning everybody, then the kidnappers will know I told the police and they could hurt or even kill David.

'What is the alternative to calling the police, Eve?' Annie asked, seeing her friend hesitate again. In fact she already suspected what the answer would be.

'That I do a bit of investigating

myself first,' Eve replied. 'You must admit I am good at it.'

'No,' Annie said firmly. 'It's much too dangerous. If the kidnappers discover what you're doing, they might hurt David . . . and you.'

'Well, I think it's a better idea than telling the police. I'm sorry, Annie, I've changed my mind. I'm going to look for David myself first.'

'If you're that determined, I'm going to help you. At least I'll be able to stop you from doing anything too reckless. I know what you're like, Eve, so don't look at me like that,' she added.

Eve was giving Annie a hurt look, but she knew her friend was right. She did tend to rush into things without thinking, but this time she had to mull over every move. After all, David's life and their future together was at stake.

* * *

An hour later, after Eve had checked both David's mobile and land line and she and Annie had gone to his house to make sure he wasn't there, Eve had to accept that the letter was genuine. There had been a huge part of her that had hoped it was a hoax, but unfortunately that didn't seem to be the case. She thought that if anybody had done it just to frighten her, the main culprit would be Betty Jones.

'So,' Annie asked. 'What are we going to do now, Eve?'

They were back in Eve's lounge and Annie was worried what Eve's next move would be.

'I think the prime suspect is Joanna Neonakis so we need to search her house, presuming she's not there of course.'

'Do you think she would keep David in her own home . . . that is if she has him of course?'

'I don't know . . . wait. He could be in the other house, the one that's currently up for sale. I wonder if it's locked?'

Eve was starting to get excited which

didn't please Annie one bit.

'I would imagine it is locked, Eve. Don't you think it would be better if I made an appointment to look around with the estate agent? If they refuse, then it's possible that Joanna has told them not to show anyone around and the chances are that David is there. Breaking in sounds awfully dangerous to me.'

'You don't have to break in. You can stay in the car and keep a lookout while I go in. However, if you're that worried, we can go to the house and see which estate agents have it on their books. We could try and get an appointment to look round. Then as you said, if they refuse, we'll know there's something fishy going on.'

Annie agreed, but she was still anxious.

* * *

Ten minutes later, Eve and Annie arrived at the house. Annie had insisted that she drove, despite Eve's protestations. However, Annie was, for once, firm with her. Eve was in no condition to drive. She was both anxious and stressed and with her in control of the car, who knew where they might end up.

There were two estate agents boards up outside the house. Annie took down both numbers and then drove a little way down the road to phone them. One didn't answer, but the other did and Annie made an appointment with them for two days' time. They said they were fully booked for the next day, while today their sales staff were taking clients elsewhere.

'That's suspicious, Annie, don't you think? Perhaps Joanna's said that nobody can view today so she can get David out of the house. What do you think?'

'I think the estate agent is just fully booked today with clients looking at other houses, just like they said. Eve, if Joanna has David and I'm not saying she has, she's put him somewhere where there's no chance of him being found. In my opinion, she's a very capable, clever woman.'

'Hmm, you're probably right, though perhaps she has him in her own house so she can keep an eye on him.'

'You'll never get in there.'

'Yes I will. I don't know how, but I will and it will be tonight. And I think it's worth breaking into this house tonight as well. They want the money in two days' time so I can't hang around.'

'We'll probably end up being arrested,' Annie said with a sigh.

'You don't have to come with me. I'm capable of doing this on my own.'

'I can't leave you to do this alone, Eve. I'd never forgive myself if anything happened to you. All that I insist on is that we come back when it's dark. You could easily be seen in daylight. I've noticed a few people walking about.'

'Whatever,' Eve replied, but inside she was relieved. She was a little nervous of breaking in to two houses and was glad Annie was coming with her.

5

That evening at eight thirty, Annie picked up Eve. Eve had had an awful afternoon and hadn't been able to settle down to doing anything productive at all. She tried to go through all her finances, but so much of her money was tied up in different investments and she knew she wouldn't be able to get anywhere near 100,000 Euros in cash within two days.

Eve was desperate to rescue David and tried to think who else could have kidnapped him, but she couldn't believe it was anyone else she knew. They were all friends of hers and of David's, apart from Betty, but she couldn't see her kidnapping anyone at her age. It had to be Joanna and an accomplice; but whether that person was Kevin or someone else, she was unsure.

Eventually Eve drifted off to sleep

and when she woke up, it was already almost eight. She realised that she hadn't eaten all day and now there wasn't time. Grabbing a packet of crisps, she hoped it would be enough to sustain her, and she then went and redid her make-up. She also changed into a black top and black leggings. Eve remembered doing the same when she and David had broken into Phyllis Baldwin's house the previous summer and discovered evidence that she was the killer of Jane's father.

Eve's eyes welled up with tears as she remembered David. Would she ever be able to do anything like this with him again? And more importantly, would they be able to get married? Eve tried desperately to pull herself together.

I'll be no good to David if I'm an emotional wreck, nor will I find him if I don't concentrate. Our future is at stake and I won't let that awful woman, Joanna, take it away from us.

By the time the door bell rang, Eve had composed herself and was ready to do whatever was needed to get David back. Annie however, was uncertain that this was the best way to go about it.

'Are you sure you want to do this, Eve? It's very risky.'

'Of course I do. You can stay in the car and keep a lookout. Phone me if Joanna comes.'

Annie nodded, still not happy about what they were going to do. She was also feeling guilty about lying to her husband. She had said she was having a girl's night in with Eve and he had believed her. She felt terrible, especially as he had been a police officer. What would he say if he knew what they were up to?

* * *

Eve and Annie drove to the house that was up for sale first. It was an older house inside a village and had belonged to the parents of Yiannis. There was nobody about in the village and Eve was relieved. Still, she got out of the car quickly and closed the door as quietly as she could before walking swiftly towards the front door. She tried the handle first, but wasn't surprised when she found that it was locked. She had a quick look under the mat, but the key wasn't there. The shutters were locked on all the windows as well and Eve felt very disappointed. Was she going to have to return home without getting in?

She decided to go round the back of the house in the hope that a window or door had been left open there. However, the shutters were all down and the door was locked. Eve was desperate enough to even think of breaking a window to get in, but without the shutters being open, she wasn't able to.

As Eve turned round from trying the door, she tripped over a flower pot and fell. She, the pot and its contents went flying.

'Damn,' she cried out, before realising how loud she'd shouted.

'What's this?' Eve whispered aloud a

moment later as she bent down to clear the mess. 'It's a key! It must have been under the flowerpot. Please let it be the one to open the back door.'

Eve got up and brushed herself down. She looked around, but nobody seemed to be coming to see what the noise was. She walked to the door and slowly put the key in the lock. Imagine her delight when it fitted! She breathed a sigh of relief as she entered the house, quietly closing the door behind her.

Eve got her torch out and flashed it around the room. She saw that she was in the kitchen. Staying there for a moment, she then moved from room to room downstairs before heading upstairs. After a few minutes, she felt less nervous and anyway, she knew Annie would ring if there was any danger. When she came downstairs again, she noticed another door and thought it must lead to the basement. Eve started to tremble, knowing that if David was in the house, he would probably be down there. The door had a key in it so Eve turned it. It opened easily so she switched on the light and went down very slowly, hoping not to fall as the stairs were steep. She didn't want to have to call emergency services from a house she had broken into!

When she got to the bottom of the stairs, she called for David, but there was no answer. She then walked around the basement, but there was nothing suspicious at all. David wasn't there and Eve couldn't contain her disappointment.

Eve went back up the stairs, making sure to switch off the light and lock the door. The only problem was the flowerpot. Luckily, there was a similar one that had been next to it, so she put the key under that one. As for the broken one, a stray cat or a beach marten could easily have knocked it over.

Eve walked cautiously to Annie's car. To her relief, there was still nobody about.

'David wasn't there,' Eve said as she

got into the car.

'Can we go home then?' Annie asked, hoping against hope that Eve wouldn't want to go to the other house.

'I know you don't want me to break into Joanna's other house, but I have to. I must see if David's there.'

'Joanna herself might be there. Then what are you going to do?'

'I've thought about that. I've decided to ring the doorbell first. Then I'll know if she's in or not.'

'But what if she answers the door? You've told me that from the brief meetings you've had, that you don't get on.'

'Well, I thought I'd tell her how silly we've been for having a feud for no real reason and invite her to a little party I'm giving a week on Saturday.'

'What will you do if she accepts, Eve?'

'If she does, I'll have to have a party I suppose, but if she has kidnapped David, I doubt if she will accept my invitation. I'll just have to watch the house to see when she goes out. I'll try and break in then.'

'Oh Eve. Please be careful.'

'I will, I promise, Annie,' she replied, crossing her fingers behind her back.

* * *

Annie then drove to Joanna's other house, neither woman saying much. Annie knew there was nothing she could do now to prevent Eve from entering the second property.

As Eve got out of the car, Annie shook her head. Where was it all going to end?

Eve had reached the front door. The shutters were closed and the front door was completely made of wood, so Eve realised that the lights could be on behind them. She took a deep breath and rang the doorbell and waited. Nobody came to the door so Eve rang again. When there was still no reply, Eve smiled.

She started to walk round the back,

but came across a fence.

Damn! Mind you, it's not that high. I'm sure I could get over it . . .

Eve put one of her feet in-between two of the pieces of wood making up the fence and then managed to get her other leg over the fence. As she then brought the first leg over, she felt a part of the fence snap and she looked at it in horror.

What have I done? I've already committed enough crimes to be put in jail. But then, what about David? Come on, Eve, pull yourself together. David's more important than a broken fence.

Once back on the ground Eve walked round the back, glad that the moon was almost full and she could see quite well. However, there were no flower pots with a back door key underneath this time. She looked under the mat and there was no key there either. The shutters each side of the kitchen door were shut, but as she looked along the house, she saw a window further along which had its shutters open. Eve breathed a sigh of relief and went to have a look.

She reached the window and tried to open it. It was locked, but it didn't seem to be very tight. It was one of John Phillips's houses and most of them had been shoddily made as Eve herself could testify, having bought one herself. She thought that if she rattled the window for long enough, it might open.

Eve started to shake the window and at first it didn't move. However, a couple of minutes later it became looser until finally it opened. Eve couldn't believe her luck, although she did make a note to have better locks fitted on her own windows. She climbed inside the house quickly, knowing that the faster she was the better. Joanna could be back at any time.

Switching on her torch, Eve saw she was in the sitting room. Thinking that the most likely place David would be was the basement, Eve went off in search of one.

Meanwhile, Annie sat in the car,

feeling sick. Amateur sleuthing was not for her and she kept thinking what her husband would say if he found out. He would not be a happy man at all.

Then a car drove up and stopped outside Joanna's house. Annie's heart missed a few beats and when she saw Joanna and Kevin get out of the car, she struggled to get hold of her mobile in her bag. She was all thumbs and wasted precious seconds finding it. However, finally Annie managed to dial Eve's mobile, but unfortunately there was no reply. Eve was, at that moment, in the basement and there was no mobile signal.

A few moments later Eve emerged, her heart heavy as she'd found nothing of interest downstairs. She'd drifted off into her own world and didn't realise that there was a light on in the hall. As she reached the top of the stairs, she came face to face with Joanna and Kevin.

There were a couple of moments of silence before Joanna spoke, unable to hide her astonishment any more.

'What on earth are you doing in my house, Eve Masters?' she asked frostily, not for one minute losing her cool. 'How dare you break into my home! I thought you were a rich woman, or perhaps you weren't stealing . . . but snooping.'

Eve was feeling sick.

Why on earth didn't Annie phone me to say they were coming home? She had to think quickly.

'Where is David?' Eve asked firmly, not allowing herself to stumble over her words. 'I know you've got him somewhere and you'd better tell me where he is.'

Joanna sounded mystified by Eve's words.

'I have absolutely no idea what you're going on about, Eve. How would I know where David is? Have you gone crazy?'

'Ha, don't give me that!' Eve replied. 'I know it was you who kidnapped David and sent me the ransom note. I'll tell you this, there's no way I can get that amount of money by Friday.'

Joanna stared at Eve in horror. 'I'm sorry about David,' she said, 'but I'm very put out that you're accusing me. Why on earth would I want to kidnap David?'

'For the money of course,' Eve replied.

'I have plenty of money, thank you,' Joanna remarked, smiling.

'Oh, you can never have too much money,' Eve commented, trying to keep her cool.

'I'm sorry, Eve, but I'm going to have to call the police. I have no choice.'

'Really? Is that necessary?' Kevin finally joined in the conversation.

'Yes, yes I think so. She can't break into my house and get away with it.'

'But the person who kidnapped David said there had to be no police involved. They could kill him, or you could. As I couldn't get the money I had no choice but to look for him myself.'

'Oh, for heavens sake, Eve,' Joanna snapped, 'I haven't got David. Anyway, he's much more important to his kidnappers alive than dead.'

'Call the police if you will, but then David will die if I'm left in a police cell.'

'I don't really care what happens to you, Eve Masters, but I care very much that you broke into my house and you're not getting away with it. Excuse me for one moment.'

While she was gone, Eve spoke to Kevin.

'Thanks for nothing, Kevin. You could have stood up for me a bit more than you did.'

'It wouldn't have done any good. I doubt she would be swayed by anyone.'

'Not even you? You seem to have got quite friendly lately.'

'We have. It came as quite a surprise to me, but of course Lucy and I hadn't been close for a long time.'

'What about Joanna? She had only recently married Yiannis.'

'She now thinks it was more of an infatuation.'

'Well,' Joanna said coming back into the hallway. 'Chief Police Officer Dimitris Kastrinakis will be here soon. We'd better wait in the lounge.'

Eve breathed a sigh of relief. Dimitris Kastrinakis had been the officer in charge of all the murders and knew her well. He would know that she hadn't been trying to rob Joanna's house. However, he had continually told her to keep her nose out of police business, but she had kept ignoring him. He would be really angry that she had taken the law into her own hands yet another time.

* * *

They sat in the lounge for over twenty minutes before Dimitris arrived, barely saying a word to each other. However, all their minds were active.

Eve was still thinking that Joanna was

the most likely person to have kidnapped David, but where else could she have put him? She wasn't physically strong enough to overpower him, so who was her partner? Perhaps it was Kevin, or maybe there was someone else and she was also planning an untimely end for Kevin?

Kevin himself was a little worried. If Eve was right, perhaps Joanna was going out with him with a plan to marry him and then kill him for his money. After all, she did get over Yiannis very quickly. However, he dismissed this idea almost as soon as it had come to him.

Joanna just wished the police would arrive and take away that infernal busybody. She did wonder however what the police would actually do with Eve. They would probably believe her; nobody would make up something like that, but she still shouldn't have broken into her home. Joanna decided that she probably wouldn't press charges in the end; her main aim was to give Eve a fright.

When the doorbell finally rang, Eve jumped and her heart started racing. All she knew was that she'd never survive jail, especially knowing that it would waste valuable time which she needed to spend looking for David. This stupidity of hers could cost him his life.

A few moments later, Joanna came back in with Dimitris and another policeman.

'Well, well, well, Miss Masters,' Dimitris said. 'Turned to robbery now, have you?'

Kevin stifled a laugh and Joanna shot him a dirty look.

'I wasn't trying to steal anything, sir,' Eve stated, attempting to sound firm. 'I was looking for my fiancé, David Baker. He has been kidnapped and the kidnappers want 100,000 Euros. I have most of my money invested and I can't get it all in cash quickly enough.'

'And may I ask why you think Joanna Neonakis has kidnapped him?'

'She doesn't like me for a start . . . '

'I am oblivious to your presence,' Joanna butted in.

'You were flirting with David at the airport while ignoring me. Decent women don't do that.'

'You were chasing after another man, Joanna?' Kevin asked.

'It was harmless flirtation, for goodness sake, Kevin. I flirt all the time, but that doesn't mean I'm interested.'

'Come now,' Dimitris said. 'We're going off the subject completely. Eve, couldn't you come and talk to the police instead of breaking into Joanna's house?'

'The letter said not to go to the police.'

'Well,' Joanna interrupted once again, 'you must be worried now, Eve. If you think I'm the kidnapper, it would have been me who told you not to go to the police and here you are talking to them.'

'I didn't go to them though, did I? You called the police,' Eve said smugly.

'Now, now, we'll have none of this

bickering,' Dimitris put in.

'By the way, Eve,' Joanna said. 'Did you go to my other house?'

All eyes shifted to Eve who now looked uncomfortable and very sheepish.

'Well, yes, but I didn't have to break in as there was a key under a flowerpot in the back garden.'

She omitted to mention that she had broken the flowerpot.

'David wasn't there either,' Eve added, 'but she could have found somewhere much safer to put him.'

'I'm telling you that I didn't kidnap him,' Joanna screamed, finally losing her cool.

'Shut up, both of you, or I will arrest you, Joanna, as well as Eve,' Dimitris said.

Joanna became silent straight away and Eve said nothing. Kevin sat with his head in his hands, thinking that this was not what he had signed up for. His marriage had ended up being miserable. Then he thought he'd found a wonderful, beautiful woman who cared for him as he did for her, but she was bringing too many complications into his life. He wanted a simple existence after all he'd been through.

'Right,' Dimitris spoke. 'Mrs Neonakis, do you want to press charges against Eve for breaking and entering?'

Joanna looked directly at Eve. Yes, she wanted to. She didn't like Eve at all, although she didn't know why; possibly because they were very similar. Both women were beautiful, strong women who liked power. Joanna had imagined stealing David from Eve; in fact nothing would give her greater pleasure.

'No, no I won't press charges,' she finally said. 'Eve has more important things to worry about at the moment.'

Eve was surprised by Joanna's reply.

'Thank you, Joanna,' she said, but thought immediately afterwards that there must be an ulterior motive.

'We won't keep you any longer then, Mrs Neonakis, Mr Fowler. Good night.'

As Eve went out the door with

Dimitris and the other officer, he asked her where her car was. Luckily, Eve was able to think quickly in most situations and this time wasn't an exception.

'I walked. It would have been silly to bring the car, wouldn't it?'

Dimitris nodded in agreement while Eve sighed in relief that he couldn't see her blushing. She was also relieved that Annie had gone and thought she must have left after the police arrived. It would have been stupid for her to get into trouble as well. She only hoped Annie wouldn't phone until she was back home and on her own.

'Right,' Dimitris said. 'We'll take you home, Miss Masters. By the way, we'll need the ransom letter. Tomorrow you'll need to come down to the station to make a statement about the break-in.'

'But what if the kidnappers see me, Inspector? They said no police and if they're watching, they could kill David.'

'Very well, we can leave your statement on the break-in for a couple of days. Apart from Joanna, do you have any idea who could have kidnapped Mr Baker?'

'No, none at all. Everybody else are our friends, well expect for Betty Jones and I can't see her having the strength to overpower David.'

'Do you know anyone, perhaps with financial problems, who may have been led to do this through desperation?'

Eve thought long and hard.

'Well, I can, but I doubt that these people would have done it.'

'You must tell me. Anything will help.'

'Alright,' Eve spoke reluctantly. 'There's Ken and Jan who own The Black Cat. They think they might have to go back to England because of all the extra taxes they have to pay. They don't want to go, but they need a lot more money.'

'Is there anyone else?'

'Don Jones wants to divorce Betty, but they're broke apart from the house. I can't see him having the strength, unless of course he has an accomplice . . . And that's it, I think.'

'You know the kidnappers could be watching you now, Miss Masters?' Dimitris said.

'Then it could be too late for David. What am I to do, Inspector?' Eve asked, feeling at a complete loss.

Dimitris was surprised to see Eve so devoid of hope. She was obviously very worried about David and 100,000 Euros was a lot of money. Dimitris suspected that she had more than enough cash to pay it, but who would want to give away money they had worked hard for?

'Listen,' Dimitris said, trying to sound upbeat. 'I doubt if the kidnappers are around now and if they are, there's not much we can do about it. I will drive you home, look at the letter and as I have my sergeant with me, take a statement tonight. How's that?'

Eve nodded in agreement and got into the back of the car. Her mind racing, they had an almost silent journey back to her house.

At one point Dimitris did start talking to his sergeant who Eve learnt was called Stavros, and Eve took advantage of that time to fiddle in her bag and discreetly switch her phone off just in case Annie called. She didn't want to get her friend into trouble and it would be very difficult to talk to her without giving anything away.

* * *

Once the officers and Eve had left her house, Joanna said goodnight to Kevin, or at least she tried to.

'Darling, I'm tired. It's time you went home. It was a lovely meal in Bella Sophia, if only that woman hadn't broken in afterwards and ruined the evening. Eve has stressed me out and I do need to go to bed now.'

'Why won't you let me stay, Joanna? I'm in love with you, you know I am. How long are you going to keep me waiting?' Kevin pleaded.

He was a little drunk, not normally having the nerve to ask Joanna outright if he could spend the night with her.

'You know I have to take this slowly. You didn't love your wife. I did love Yiannis and I don't feel quite right rushing straight into another relationship. I feel a bit guilty to tell you the truth, but I can't resist you, you know that. Please take it at my pace. You won't regret it.'

'Alright, you know I'll do anything you say; I can't help it. Will I see you tomorrow?'

'Of course. I'll call you.'

Joanna sidled up to Kevin and slipped her arms around him, smiling. Kevin felt his legs turn to jelly. This woman was worth waiting for. Joanna pulled him closer and pressed her lips onto his, kissing him slowly, while running her fingers up and down his back. Kevin shivered and wished she'd never stop.

Then the kiss was suddenly over and

Joanna had moved away leaving Kevin wanting more, much more.

⋆ ⋆ ⋆

Not long after leaving Joanna's house, Dimitris and Stavros were sitting in Eve's lounge while she got them coffee. She had told them it would only be instant, hoping they'd refuse and be gone as soon as possible, but they didn't. The Greeks are very fond of their special coffee which has to be boiled in a pan, but Eve had never tried to make it.

'Right, Miss Masters,' Dimitris said as Eve came back into the lounge. 'We'll make this as painless as possible. Have you got the letter?'

'I have. It's here,' Eve replied and went to get it out of a drawer.

She handed it over and Dimitris studied it for a few minutes.

'We'll dust it for fingerprints, but my guess is that there won't be any apart from yours. I take it the letter was just pushed through the door as there is no stamp.'

'Yes, I could have seen the kidnapper myself. I was at home.'

'Unless he paid some kid to deliver it and watched from a distance.'

Eve sighed. What was wrong with her? Dimitris was being so sharp, whereas all her powers of deduction had disappeared.

'Now, Miss Masters, can you tell me why you think Mrs Neonakis is the kidnapper?'

'I've been suspicious of her from the moment I saw her. She apparently only knew Yiannis for two weeks before marrying him. She inherited two houses from him and then after his funeral, she came into The Black Cat with Kevin Fowler looking quite happy, and she did touch his hand. Now it seems they're a couple.'

'But that doesn't explain why she would kidnap Mr Baker.'

'For the money of course. She must have married Yiannis for money, she's seeing Kevin and he's not poor and she's trying to get my money, too.'

'But where is Mr Baker? He wasn't in either of her houses.'

'I don't know. He could be anywhere.'

Eve knew it all sounded far-fetched, but who else could have him?

'You know you shouldn't have broken into Mrs Neonakis's houses this evening. You're lucky she isn't pressing charges.'

'She's probably trying to make out she's innocent,' she replied sharply.

Dimitris Kastrinakis shook his head. He didn't know if there was anything he could do to stop Eve Masters searching for her fiancé, but it could be dangerous.

'You need to stop now, Miss Masters,' Dimitris said firmly. 'You must stop looking for Mr Baker. Whoever has him may kill him, don't you understand that? You must leave this to us.'

Eve said nothing. Was he right? The

letter did say that the police mustn't be involved. What could they do anyway?

'Now,' Dimitris continued, 'if the kidnappers contact you again, you must let me know immediately, do you understand?'

Eve nodded, feeling well and truly told off, but when Dimitris and Stavros had gone, she regained some of her usual composure.

I'll be damned if I leave everything to you Dimitris. You won't know where to look for my David, will you?

6

While Eve was sitting at home desperately trying to think of her next move, David was lying on a mattress trying to sleep. He didn't know what time it was, but he knew he was hungry. It had been hours since he'd had something to eat and been untied and allowed to go to the bathroom. Because his kidnapper had a gun, David hadn't dared try to escape when he'd been untied. Perhaps he'd give it a go later, but at the moment he was too scared and didn't know if he'd make it.

He didn't think they'd kill him if he made a run for it, but they could certainly hurt him, possibly quite badly to ensure he wouldn't try it again.

They hadn't told him why they had kidnapped him, but he had begun to think there could only be one reason. They wanted money, money from Eve no doubt. As he lay there, he started thinking about her again. In fact, he had thought about little else. He couldn't believe how lucky he was to have someone so beautiful and intelligent interested in him. And she wanted to marry him, but would that happen now? David was having serious doubts.

He wondered how much the kidnappers had asked for his safe return. He had no idea, but he expected it was a great deal of money. Everyone knew that Eve was well-off. She had enough money to never have to work again, but David didn't want her to spend most of it on getting him out of this mess. It was her security for the future and she had worked hard to get it.

What he was most worried about was Eve taking the law into her own hands. He had to get out of here before she did something stupid.

A moment later, David heard a key turn in the door at the top of the stairs and his kidnapper came down with a plate of food. He carried his gun and kept it firmly pointed at David while he untied his hands and then told David to untie his own feet and take the gag out of his mouth. David felt relieved for the little time he had with his feet and hands untied. They were beginning to feel decidedly painful.

'Sit up and eat,' his kidnapper spoke. 'I'm sorry I'm late. You must be hungry. By the way, don't try and make a run for it. I'm never alone.'

David looked at his kidnapper, wondering if he was telling the truth. Was there really someone else upstairs? However, he didn't want to find out. He also didn't want to beg to be released. He knew it would do no good.

David quickly scanned the man standing over him and despite the fact that he was wearing a mask, he had a feeling that he knew who he was.

That voice is so familiar. I can't believe it's him, but it does sound like him, David thought as he tucked into his bread and cheese. At least this meal was better than the brown slush that he'd had earlier.

The kidnapper moved back, deciding that it would be stupid to talk as if everything was normal. It was nothing of the sort and in a way he wished he wasn't involved. David was a good man and they had become friends, but she had promised him so much and he hadn't been able to resist her.

Ten minutes later he was gone and David was alone in the dark. He wasn't quite so afraid now, thinking that the chances of them killing him were less than he thought. The man that had come downstairs just wasn't tough enough anyway.

Eventually, David drifted off to sleep and after such a traumatic and confusing day, he had some weird dreams. Eve appeared in one of them looking as stunning as ever. They were standing on the beach wearing their swimming costumes and holding onto each other tightly. She was telling him how much she loved him and would never let him go.

A moment later their lips met in an overpowering kiss that seemed to last forever. However, they then disappeared and reappeared a moment later in their wedding outfits. He thought how amazing she looked in her long white silk dress and he reached out to her, but the more he called her name, the further from him she went until she had disappeared into the distance.

David woke up in a sweat. Was this what was going to happen? Was he never going to see Eve again? Lying there he guessed that the kidnappers had asked for more money than Eve could get her hands on. Then an awful thought struck him. Perhaps she's going to refuse to pay the ransom. She doesn't love me enough to give them the money for my release . . . and why should she? He wouldn't blame her if she didn't want to lose her savings. He'd just have to try and escape; that was the only thing he could do.

7

It was getting late, but Eve didn't want to go to bed, feeling that she wouldn't be able to sleep after such a distressing day.

As soon as Dimitris and Stavros left, she phoned Annie to tell her what had happened. Annie told her that she had phoned her when she saw the police arrive, but realised that Eve must have been out of mobile range.

After the police went into Joanna's house, Annie had driven home and hadn't called again in case Eve was still with the police. She was naturally pleased that Eve hadn't been arrested, but she was feeling extremely guilty for not telling her husband, Pete.

Eve promised not to involve her again.

As soon as Eve put the phone down, she sank back in her armchair. She suddenly felt drained and thought what a waste of a day it had been. She had been convinced that Joanna had kidnapped David and that she was going to find him, but she hadn't. It had taken all day to achieve nothing and she hadn't even started the process of releasing her funds, not that it would make any difference as it wouldn't get to her in time from England. However, perhaps if the kidnappers knew that the money was on its way, they would continue to keep David alive.

Eve definitely needed a drink, but not her favourite gin and tonic. That was her 'happy' summertime drink, sipped slowly with David sitting out on the balcony watching the sunset. She felt tears welling up and tried to think of something else, but it was no use; all she could think about was David. The tears started to fall and they wouldn't stop.

Oh, that beautiful wedding we were going to have. I can't believe that it might not happen; that David and I won't make our vows on a golden sun kissed beach. This isn't fair.

When she finally stopped crying, Eve got up and poured herself a Metaxa, the delicious sweet Greek brandy which both she and David were quite partial to. As she sipped it, the phone rang giving Eve a fright. Warily, she got up to answer it. The voice on the other end sounded strange, as if a piece of cloth or handkerchief was covering the person's mouth.

'We told you, no police.'

Eve couldn't tell if it was a man or a woman who was speaking.

'I'm sorry,' she replied quickly, not wanting to antagonise the person. 'I was arrested, so I couldn't help but see the police.'

'Trying to find David I presume.'

'I can't get so much money in such a short space of time. I had no choice but to look for David. Why won't you give me a few extra days to get the cash?'

'Very well, you get until Monday. If

you don't have the money by then, David dies.'

With that, the kidnapper put the phone down. Eve breathed a sigh of relief, but she still didn't know if she could get all the money by then.

She went and got her financial papers out and worked out that she could get 80,000 Euros within the time limit, but it was touch and go for the other 20,000. Could she borrow this from anyone? She knew that most of her friends on Crete didn't have much money, and as for her friends in England; well most of them were colleagues more than friends, except for Robert Parker. He had been one of her clients in her early days as a showbiz agent, but after they had a little fling, she decided he should get representation elsewhere. However, they remained good friends from that time on, he being one of the few people who knew how Eve's mind worked.

He was quite a successful actor now

and wasn't short of money. He had visited Eve the previous summer and had got involved in the murder inquiries. Much to Betty's chagrin, Robert and her niece, Alison Taylor, who had also been visiting Crete, had fallen for each other. Betty had spent a great deal of energy trying to push Alison towards David, not wanting Eve to capture his heart, but all her efforts were for nothing.

Eve didn't want to phone Robert, but there was nobody else. She decided there was no time like the present, so she picked up the phone and blurted out the story as soon as he answered. Finally, he was allowed to speak.

'Eve, slow down and calm down, you'll give yourself a heart attack. Of course I'll lend you the 20,000 Euros.'

'You will, oh thank you, Robert. You don't know what this means to me.'

'You've done a lot for me, Eve, and I know you're good for the money. But Eve, breaking into two houses! When will you learn? You could have been thrown into jail and wouldn't have had a chance to get the ransom money together.'

'I know. I was convinced it was Joanna and I still suspect her. Now I've got until Monday to get the money, so I still have a chance to find David.'

'Oh no, what are you going to do, Eve?'

'I don't know. Not breaking and entering, I promise, but I can't sit here doing nothing.'

'That's it. I'll get the money transferred online tonight and I'll see if I can get a flight over tomorrow. I'm not working at the moment and won't be for a couple of weeks. Somebody needs to keep an eye on you.'

'OK. It will be lovely to see you, Robert, but I'm still going to look for David, I promise you.'

'Fine, but I'll be there to stop you getting into too much trouble.'

As Robert put the phone down, images of the previous summer flashed through his mind. He remembered dancing closely with Eve at Betty and Don's party and later Eve kissing him on the beach. It was all to make David jealous. Then there was the time when Phyllis Baldwin, the murderer, tampered with the brakes on Eve's car and they went careering into a field. He wondered what surprises awaited him this time on Crete?

* * *

After leaving Eve's house, Dimitris went back to the police station and sat in his office thinking about the case. He was troubled. He'd never had to deal with a kidnapping before and felt a little out of his depth even though he would never admit it to anyone, especially not Eve Masters.

What trouble that woman has brought him in the space of just one year, but he was concerned for her now. Why, oh why, did she have to go searching for David on her own?

A few moments later, the phone rang

and Dimitris wasn't surprised that it was Eve.

'What can I do for you, Miss Masters,' he asked patiently.

Dimitris had decided to be tolerant with her now, seeing as she was going through such a difficult time.

'Don't worry,' Eve replied quickly, 'I haven't done anything stupid. The kidnapper has just been on the phone and agreed to give me until Monday to get the money together.'

'That's good. Did you recognise the voice?'

'No, but it sounded like he or she had put a hanky or something in front of his or her mouth.'

'It sounds like it's someone you know then. That narrows it down a little. Now try and get some sleep, Eve, so you are ready for the next few days.'

'OK, I'll try. Thank you, Inspector.'

As Eve put the phone down, she felt pleasantly surprised. 'Well, there's a turn-up for the books,' she said out loud. 'Dimitris is actually being polite to me. He must be concerned. Wonders will never cease!'

* * *

Meanwhile, Annie Davies was watching television, but she wasn't concentrating on the programme. She wished she'd been able to persuade Eve not to break into Joanna's houses, but what could anyone do when Eve had made up her mind?

She didn't think she'd sleep that night worrying about it. What if Eve had been arrested? What if she herself had been seen and arrested as well? Pete would not have been happy. In fact, he'd have been very angry with her for breaking the law. And now Eve was no further forward in finding David and she had lost a day when she could have sorted out the money for the ransom.

'I'm just popping down to the shop for milk,' Pete said, coming into the lounge. 'There's not enough for breakfast.'

'What? Oh, milk? OK.'

'Are you alright, Annie? You've seemed distracted since you got back from Eve's.'

'Have I? I'm sorry, darling, I'm just tired. I think I'll have an early night tonight.'

'Probably do you good,' Pete replied, kissing the top of her head.

Annie watched her husband leave, feeling even more guilty. They never kept secrets from each other. Perhaps she should tell him what she had been up to this evening after all, but he would be so cross; she knew he would. He had been a police officer and he had always followed the letter of the law. No, it was for the best that she didn't tell him, but what if someone had seen her drop off Eve at either of the houses? That person could tell Pete and it would be worse coming from somebody else rather than from her. The whole thing was making her a nervous wreck.

With that Annie decided to go to bed. It was getting late and she didn't want to be around when Pete got back from the shop otherwise she might be tempted to tell him. She would hopefully be asleep by the time he came up. With any luck, tomorrow her head might be clearer.

* * *

Eve didn't want to go to bed, knowing that she probably wouldn't be able to sleep. She kept thinking about David, imagining that he was tied up somewhere dark and dismal, not knowing what was going to happen to him. She longed for him to be beside her now.

They would often curl up on the couch in the evening, his strong, comforting arms around her, making her feel safe and secure. She couldn't express how much she needed to feel protected now and to have David with her. She could almost smell his aromatic aftershave which always lingered even after he had left her. She closed her eyes and could almost see his face. She imagined him running his fingers up and down her back before kissing her neck gently and then . . .

As the tears welled up again, Eve jumped up and got another drink. She had to stop thinking of David otherwise she would fall apart. She put on the television and tried to concentrate on what was on, but images of David still kept popping up in her mind.

Eve finally went to bed at midnight, aware that she probably wasn't going to get much sleep. However, the mental and physical trials of the day had tired her out so much that she fell asleep almost as soon as her head hit the pillow.

8

That same evening was a very quiet one in The Black Cat. In fact, the only customers were Betty and Don Jones who were sitting together at a corner table. They hadn't said much to each other in the hour they had already been there. Don finally spoke.

'Do you want another drink, Betty?'

'There's not much point, is there? You've hardly said a word to me this evening; in fact you've hardly talked to me properly in days. Is there someone else?'

'Oh no, not this again, Betty. Please don't let us have an argument in public. You were convinced I was having an affair with Lucy Fowler, but I wasn't. Can't you accept that we've just grown bored with each other?'

'I haven't got bored with you. You're bored with me. And it hardly matters if we have an argument in here. We're the only customers.'

'Whatever, Betty. You used to like to have a bit of fun, but all that's gone. You're miserable and you seem hell bent on making enemies wherever you go. I want a divorce.'

Don couldn't believe he had finally asked his wife for a divorce, but now he had said the words, he wasn't going to take them back.

'What?' Betty exclaimed. 'No, I'm not giving you a divorce. You don't mean it. I know you don't. We've been together for forty-five years. Don't throw them away for some trollop.'

'There isn't anyone else. I just don't love you any more, Betty; it's as simple as that.'

Betty was relieved now that there was nobody else in the bar. Earlier she had wished that there had been some friend they could have chatted to. She had hoped that Annie Davies might have come in; she was so easy to talk to.

Now Betty felt close to tears, but it

wasn't because she was going to lose Don. She was more worried about what people might think.

'We'll be the laughing stock of the village, Don. People our age getting divorced. What are we going to do about the house? We'll probably never sell it with all the problems here in Greece.'

'I've thought of that. You can live there. I'll rent a room somewhere. Rooms are cheap for long term rentals and my needs are modest.'

My God. He's thought all this out. There must be someone else. He's lying, I know he is.

'I think we should go,' Don continued, seeing Betty starting to cry.

Betty nodded. She hated making a scene in public, but she hadn't finished with Don yet.

* * *

'Betty looked as if she were about to explode one minute and then cry the next,' Ken said to his wife, Jan, as they stood behind the bar.

'I didn't notice,' she replied.

'I wonder what it was all about,' he continued.

Jan shrugged her shoulders, thinking that they had more serious things to worry about than Betty and Don.

'What's up, Jan?'

'We've had yet another quiet night. How are we going to pay all those bills?'

'I'm sure it'll be better tomorrow; don't worry.'

'How can I not worry, Ken?' Jan suddenly exploded. 'This is our bread and butter. We have to do something spectacular to get the money flowing in. You don't seem that bothered and I don't know why. Perhaps you want to go back to England, but I don't.'

She stormed off into the kitchen while Ken just stood there. Of course he was worried, very worried, but he put on a brave face for Jan's sake. He hadn't thought she was aware of how bad their problems were, but he was wrong.

A moment later the door opened and Wayne Fowler came in.

'Pint of the usual, mate.'

'How's business?' Ken asked.

'Not bad at all. You?'

'Quiet as you can see. We've got to do something about it.'

'What about hosting quiz nights, karaokes, stuff like that.'

'I was thinking along those lines. People seem to like entertainment they can get involved in.'

Jan came out looking calmer and greeted Wayne with a smile.

'Has my dad been in tonight,' Wayne asked.

'Yes, at about six,' Jan replied.

'I suppose he was with that . . . that woman,' Wayne seethed.

'If you mean Joanna Neonakis,' Jan said, 'yes, he was.'

'I was hoping she'd never come back, but here she is again and flirting with my dad all the time. I can't see what she sees in him. I mean he's old enough to be her father. She's after something, mark my words.'

With that, Wayne went and sat down.

'He really doesn't like Joanna, does he?' Ken asked Jan, not waiting for an answer. 'He obviously thinks she's too young for his dad, not to mention that it's too soon after his mum died.'

Ken paused for a moment.

'Will you be alright, Jan, while I pop to the shop to get some eggs and a few other things for tomorrow morning?'

'I'll be fine, Ken. We're hardly rushed off our feet,' Jan replied miserably. 'I just hope we'll have some customers at breakfast time.'

She sat down to read a magazine having put the dishwasher on already. It didn't look like they would be open very late that evening.

* * *

Don and Betty drove home in silence, but when they got in, he spoke immediately.

'I think we should sit down and

discuss the situation and where we go from here, Betty.'

'Well, I don't want to. You've made your position very clear. That's all I need to know. Go and see a lawyer. I'm tired and I'm going to bed. You can sleep in the spare room.'

Don watched Betty walk up the stairs. This was too easy. Betty was bound to do something nasty. It was in her nature. It was worth it though, as long as he was rid of her.

9

The following day, Eve woke at eight and stretched out. For a moment she couldn't remember what had happened the previous day and wondered whether or not to go to the beach that morning. Then it hit her. David had been kidnapped and she had to free him.

That is if they haven't killed him already.

Eve sat up in bed, shaking. Kidnappers were capable of anything.

Then a thought struck her.

What if David knows who they are? They can't just let him go as he'll tell the police. I suppose they could have disguised themselves, but what if he can still tell who they are? If David's got any sense he'll pretend that he doesn't know them. Or perhaps they intend to hand him over to me, take the money and then shoot him a moment later anyway.

Eve decided all this thinking was doing her no good so she got up to make herself some coffee. She usually needed at least two cups before she could think straight. She grabbed her mobile and went downstairs. Then she had yet another thought. The kidnappers must be people she knew, otherwise how would they know her mobile number, unless of course they had persuaded David to give it to them.

As soon as Eve had sat down with a steaming mug of black coffee, her mobile rang. When she looked at the caller ID and saw it was Annie, she was relieved.

'Annie, I'm glad it's you. I had a horrible feeling it might be one of the kidnappers again.'

'No, it's just me. How are you? I've had a terrible night worrying about you.'

'Don't be concerned. I've promised Dimitris Kastrinakis that I won't go searching for David any more.'

'And do you mean it this time, Eve?'

'Of course I do, Annie. I was very nearly arrested yesterday and how could I have sorted out the money from jail? David could have died because of me.'

Annie didn't say anything, but although Eve did sound sincere, she had an awful feeling that she probably wasn't telling the truth. She couldn't imagine Eve sitting back and doing nothing while David was locked up somewhere awful.

'Well, mind you don't do anything,' Annie said quite severely. 'It could all have ended very badly yesterday, Eve. Anyway, are you able to get all the money you need?'

'With the extra time the kidnappers have given me, I can get hold of most of it and my friend, Robert, is lending me the rest. You remember him, don't you?'

'Yes, of course. As I recall, he was a very pleasant man.'

'He is, Annie. Mind you, he did say

he was going to try and get a flight over here today to keep an eye on me. I don't really need it, but it will be nice to have someone in the house to keep my mind off David.'

'I think it's a brilliant idea!' Annie exclaimed.

'Humph!' Eve snorted. 'You just think he's going to keep me in line, don't you? We'll see. By the way, Pete doesn't suspect anything, does he? You haven't confided in him?'

'No, I haven't told him anything and I'm certain he'd speak out if he did think there was something funny going on.'

Eve felt a little guilty for involving Annie. Perhaps she should have got Jane to come with her, but as nice as Jane was, she was also a frightened little mouse.

'Don't worry, I won't ask you to do anything more. Hopefully I'll have Robert to look after me.'

As soon as Eve put the phone down, it rang again. Eve, certain it was one of the kidnappers this time, picked it up tentatively.

'Eve, it's Robert. Good news. I've managed to get a seat on a plane today. I'll be at Chania airport at five this afternoon.'

'Great,' Eve replied. 'I'll be waiting for you.'

* * *

Eve spent the morning going through her finances one more time, making sure that the money would be in place if she had to hand it over to the kidnappers. However, she still refused to give up on the idea of rescuing David without giving up her money. After all, she had worked hard for it.

When she had finished, she decided to get her fridge and freezer stocked up for her visitor's arrival. Robert had a healthy appetite and even if they ate out, he'd want snacks at other times.

By the time she had done her shopping it was a quarter past two and

Eve was thankful that she hadn't had time to think about David too much. She decided to take her dog, Portia, out for a walk before heading for the airport.

About ten minutes later, Eve saw Jane walking towards her and she slowed down. What was she going to say to her? Had she heard anything about David being kidnapped? Perhaps Kevin or Joanna had spread the news of her breaking into Joanna's houses? Eve decided to let Jane take the lead in the conversation, just to see if she knew anything at all.

'Jane, hi, how are you today?' Eve asked.

'A little stressed, I'm afraid. I'm starting to sort out everything for my move back to England. You wouldn't believe how much stuff I've accumulated since I got here. I only came with one case.'

'Yes, it's amazing how much you can buy without even thinking,' Eve remarked, pleased that Jane didn't sound like she knew anything about what she had been up to the day before.

'Are you going to The Black Cat tonight, Eve?' Jane asked. 'I think I'll need a drink after all this hard work.'

'Probably. You remember my friend, Robert?'

Jane nodded.

'Well, he's coming over for a few days. I expect we'll pop in there tonight. I'll give you a call and let you know.'

'Thanks. You know I don't like going places like that on my own.'

Eve smiled. It never bothered her going anywhere by herself.

As Eve said goodbye to Jane, she started to wonder what she would say about David's absence. Perhaps they shouldn't go after all, but then it could be interesting. Perhaps the kidnappers might be there and they could give something away. No, she had to go. She'd say David was busy working on his book.

Or perhaps not. I'm always saying that, especially when we've had a fight. I'll say he's ill. Yes, that's a good one. David can be sick today.

* * *

Unfortunately, Eve had got the state of David's health chillingly right. David wasn't well at all. That morning when he had woken up, his chest hurt and he had trouble breathing.

He desperately needed a drink of water, but his kidnapper was late again. He tried to sit up, but he felt too weak.

At last he heard a key in the door upstairs and his kidnapper came down. He was still wearing that infernal mask. David wondered if he should tell him that he knew who he was so it was pointless wearing the mask, but decided against it. It could give the kidnapper a reason to kill him.

Looking at David, the kidnapper spoke.

'What's wrong with you?' he asked

after removing David's gag.

He tried to remain harsh and aloof, but he just missed the mark. Kidnapping someone you knew wasn't that easy.

'I'm getting a cold, that's all.'

'Well, don't die. Eve won't pay for a corpse.'

He tried to keep it light-hearted, but David didn't smile. Eve must be worried sick and that was no reason for laughter.

The kidnapper untied David and let him go to the bathroom, after which he was given some food and water. David felt a little better after having a drink.

'Do you need any medicine?'

'No,' David replied. 'As I said, it's just a cold.'

The kidnapper nodded and after tying him up again, left without saying anything else. David didn't want to talk either. What was there to say? He had been betrayed by a friend and he had nothing to say to him now or ever again. David curled up in a ball and went back to sleep.

* * *

At five o'clock, Eve stood at Chania airport waiting for Robert. She had looked at the arrivals board and the plane was due in on time. She suddenly remembered standing there just after Christmas the previous year waiting for Robert and his girlfriend, Alison, Betty's niece, to arrive for a holiday. However, David was by her side that time. A couple of tears rolled down her cheeks and she brushed them away quickly.

Robert saw Eve before she saw him. She looked as stunning as ever. Eve had on a tight fitting peach coloured sundress which showed off her perfect figure. Her shoulder length blonde hair shone beautifully and her perfectly applied make-up accentuated her features. However, he noticed a deep sadness in those emerald green eyes of hers and he knew he would have to be very gentle with her during this visit.

'Eve, darling, how wonderful to see you,' Robert exclaimed, throwing his arms around her.

Eve reciprocated, very happy to have her old friend with her for support.

'Oh I am pleased to see you, Robert,' she said, hugging him tightly. There's nothing like your best friend when you're in trouble.'

'Come on, Eve, let's get back to your house and you can tell me everything.'

* * *

That evening, Eve and Robert decided that they would go to The Black Cat. Robert was relieved that so far, Eve hadn't suggested that they went searching for David.

They decided to walk so that they could both have a drink and they collected Jane on the way.

Jane didn't bat an eyelid when Eve said David was ill. Eve gave strict instructions to Robert not to tell Jane about David's true predicament; in fact she told him not to mention David at all to anyone. Robert had a tendency to let things slip if he wasn't careful.

Entering the bar, Eve saw Don sitting alone. There was only one drink in front of him so she presumed that Betty wasn't there. She told the others to get the drinks in while she went to have a quick word.

'Don, hello, what are you doing sitting her all on your own?'

'Eve, good evening. I did it! I told Betty I wanted a divorce.'

'My goodness Don, well done,' Eve exclaimed. 'What did she say?'

'First she said she wouldn't give me a divorce; later she told me to go and see my solicitor. That was last night. She refused to speak to me in the morning; well apart from telling me to find my own place to live. So I went and got a hotel room for a few nights while I'm looking for rooms.'

'And have you found anywhere?'

'No, I haven't found anywhere cheap enough. But I'll look tomorrow. I feel so free, Eve.'

'I can imagine you do.'

Jane and Robert came over with the drinks.

'Are we sitting here?' Jane asked.

'I would love to share your company,' Don replied cheerfully.

'Then yes,' Eve said. 'You remember Robert, don't you?'

'Of course,' Don said, nodding to Robert. 'How long are you here for?'

'Oh, just a few days.'

'I think I'd better tell you then, seeing as you're dating Betty's niece; we've split up. I've asked for a divorce.'

'Oh,' Robert said. 'Don't tell Alison I said this, but I don't know how you stayed with her for as long as you did.'

Everybody laughed, even Eve, who was half studying the people in the room. There weren't many again. She looked over at the bar. Jan was on her own that evening, but it didn't seem to matter as it was so quiet.

The thought crossed Eve's mind that Ken and Jan could be the kidnappers. Ken had said they were struggling because of all the extra taxes. They would need money fast to pay them.

Now where could they have put David? In their cellar? Did they even have a cellar or basement?

'Earth to Eve,' she heard Robert say. 'You seem miles away.'

'I'm sorry,' Eve said, shaking her head. 'I was thinking about something . . . very rude of me. Now what were you saying?'

'Don has just told me more about him and Betty. I should phone Alison.'

'Perhaps Betty's called her already.'

'I doubt it,' Don said. 'At the moment she doesn't want to tell anyone. She feels embarrassed, or so she says. I expect that when she's calmed down, she'll want to shout out to the world how much I've wronged her.'

'Yes, that would be Betty all over,'

Eve put in. 'Robert, I think you're right. You should tell Alison. I know Betty and I can't stand each other, but it must be a difficult time for her and she'd be better off talking to someone close who might calm her down. Goodness knows what she might do if she sits brooding all on her own.'

Robert nodded and went outside to make the call in private.

'Oh dear,' Don said, looking worried. 'I'm starting to feel a little guilty about Betty. How will she cope on her own?'

'Don, she'll cope very well,' Eve exclaimed. 'She's suffering from hurt pride now, that's all. I know what I said, but I wasn't suggesting you go back to her. Betty is a strong woman and she'll get through it. You deserve to be happy, Don, and you weren't with Betty, were you?'

'No, Eve, I haven't been for a long time, and to tell the truth, I don't think she's been happy with me either.'

'Well, there you go. This is all for the best. Now you've both got a chance for some happiness.'

Jane said nothing. She was thinking how much had changed since she had arrived on Crete the previous December.

She had fallen in love with two murderers, but it hadn't put her off love. It had actually made her a stronger person and she still hoped to find that perfect man. However, she was finding it hard to believe that Don and Betty had really separated, but in a way she was pleased. Don deserved to find a kinder and more caring woman. Jane remembered when Betty had been nasty to her during the Christmas period. Eve had done a wonderful make-over on her, but Betty didn't like it and was quite cruel. She was always spiteful towards Eve; although Eve could give as good as she got. However, Betty had even managed to alienate David and Jane thought that it served her right.

Robert came back in and sat down.

'Well, Alison's going to try and get

over tomorrow or the next day. It's quiet at work so she thinks she may get a few days leave.'

'She's not going to try and reunite me and Betty, is she?' Don gasped in horror.

'No, of course not. She just wants to be there for Betty.'

'It's probably for the best then.'

'It'll cost you a fortune to stay in a hotel for too long, Don,' Robert put in.

Eve said nothing. Under normal circumstances she would have offered Don a room in her house, to hell with what Betty would have said. However, if Don stayed with her, he'd wonder where David was and she didn't want anyone else to know about the kidnapping.

'I have a perfect solution,' Jane announced, surprising everybody at the table. They all turned to look at her.

'If you stay in a hotel for just a few nights, then you can move into my house when I've gone back to England.

It's up for sale, but I doubt it will go quickly. You'd be doing me a favour — I'm not that happy leaving it empty. Only thing is that you'd have to agree to prospective buyers being shown round the place.'

'Jane, thank you,' Don replied. 'That'll suit me down to the ground. You're an absolute lifesaver.'

* * *

Two hours and a few drinks later, Eve got up to use the loo. She hadn't eaten a great deal that day and was feeling slightly tipsy. As she approached the ladies, she took a little detour, wondering where the basement was. As she was looking, she bumped into Jan.

'Can I help you, Eve?'

'Oh, I am sorry,' Eve said quickly, thinking on her feet as usual. 'I haven't eaten much today and I must admit I am a little drunk. Good job you found me, otherwise I could have fallen down your cellar stairs!'

'Good job we haven't got a cellar or basement then,' Jan replied.

Eve laughed and quickly changed the subject.

'Are you still doing food tonight?'

'Yes, for another half an hour, but only simple things like sandwiches, burgers and quiche.'

'Well, I'd better hurry up and order something.'

Jan smiled, wondering what Eve was up to. She never seemed to succumb to alcohol, even when she'd had a lot more than she'd had this evening.

Eve went into the ladies and sobered up immediately.

Well, if Ken and Jan have David, he's certainly not here. I'm beginning to think that whoever's taken him has put him somewhere where nobody would think of looking. This is getting harder and harder. I don't think I'm ever going to find him.

* * *

Meanwhile, David had just woken up. Nobody had come to see him during the day and he was dying of thirst again. The kidnapper had left the bottle of water, but he was gagged and tied up so how on earth he was supposed to drink it, heaven only knew.

He had slept nearly all day and he actually felt a little better. There had been a couple of incidents when he'd had trouble breathing, but it had been a while since the last one. He thought he would be alright if only he could get a drink of water.

As if answering his prayers, he heard the key turn in the lock upstairs and he sighed with relief as his kidnapper came downstairs and untied him and took out his gag.

'Thank goodness,' David said. 'I'm dying for a drink of water.'

'I left you the bottle,' the kidnapper snapped.

'And how would you suggest I drink from it with my hands tied up and my mouth gagged?'

'Sorry, I wasn't thinking,' the kidnapper replied, feeling guilty but trying to sound firm.

He wished his accomplice was doing this, but she had refused. He hated staring at David like this. He quickly untied him and gave him some food and water and then waited while he went to the bathroom.

As David got up, he felt a little dodgy on his legs, but he didn't feel quite as bad as he had that morning, especially as he had now had a drink. What he wouldn't do for a shot or two of whisky. That would do him the world of good.

A couple of minutes later, David came out of the bathroom and as he did, his kidnapper seemed lost in thought, his gun pointing downwards.

It's now or never, thought David as he lunged towards the other man. He didn't know where his strength came from, but he kept going, fighting back against the burning pain in his lungs.

The kidnapper didn't have time to pull his gun up, but struggled with

David, trying to push him away so that he could point the gun at him and regain control. However, physically David was a fitter man, having spent many hours in the gym. However, he started to flag, his breathing becoming difficult, and the other man seemed to be regaining control. Luckily, with what he felt was his last burst of strength, David managed to knock his kidnapper down and the man hit his head on the concrete wall. He dropped the gun and went out cold.

Despite his breathing coming in short bursts, David didn't waste a moment. This was his chance to escape, but there was only one way out of the basement and that was up the stairs.

What if the man's partner was up there? He could take the gun, but would he have the nerve to use it? He didn't think so, but he could threaten with it. However, whoever was upstairs might be cleverer and more ruthless.

He grabbed the gun. He knew that he had to go and go quickly just in case the man woke up. He hadn't planned this; it was decided on the spur of the moment and he had to go through with it. It was his only chance.

Forgetting for that moment how ill he felt, David quickly dashed up the stairs and listened at the door for a moment; it wasn't quite shut. He heard nothing so he slowly and nervously opened it. Unfortunately, it creaked and he held his breath expecting someone to pounce on him. To his relief, no one did.

David looked around the room. There was nobody there and he was more than happy when he saw that the key had been left in the door. David shut the door quickly and locked it.

He looked around, realising that it was quite a small, new house. One of the shutters had been left open and he could tell he was in the sitting room and the front door was ahead. It didn't look as if anyone lived in the house.

Worrying that the kidnapper's accomplice might be outside, David found the kitchen at the back and to his delight, the door wasn't locked. He put the gun in his pocket, went outside and ran. It was only when he got outside that he realised he should have lifted his kidnapper's mask, just to confirm his suspicions, but it was too late. It would be stupid to go back now.

* * *

Eve and Robert got back home from The Black Cat reasonably early that night. Robert was quite tired after getting up at the crack of dawn to catch his flight.

They walked Jane home first, Eve having to do everything in her power not to tell Jane about David. Jane was such a good friend and she'd even helped Eve in her search for the murderer earlier in the summer, but the less people that knew the better.

'Well, Robert,' Eve said as soon as they got in. 'I discovered that Ken and

Jan don't have a basement, so if they've kidnapped David, they're keeping him elsewhere.'

'Oh, I can't imagine them kidnapping anybody.'

'Me neither, but business hasn't been too good and they are struggling financially. They could be desperate enough.'

'Well, perhaps,' Robert replied. 'Have you completely given up on Joanna?'

'No, she's still my number one suspect.'

'With or without Kevin?'

'I'm not sure. Could be with him, or she might have another accomplice.'

'Well, on that note, I think I'll be off to bed. I feel shattered.'

'OK, Robert. Thanks so much for coming over.'

'It's a pleasure. Now don't stay up too long thinking about David.'

Eve nodded, but she didn't think she could help herself.

* * *

David ran and ran, but suddenly he had to stop. He felt sick and dizzy. His head was spinning and he was wheezing. What was the matter with him? He had felt better, but after the fight and all this running, he was feeling terrible.

He wasn't quite sure where he was, but he knew he had to keep going, despite feeling wretched. He decided it might be better to walk now rather than run. At least he might make it to a police station.

However, a few minutes later, his legs felt like jelly and he knew he had to rest. Seeing an olive grove, he went in as far away from the road as possible and lay down, just to rest for a little while and get his strength back.

10

In the basement where David had been held captive, his kidnapper finally stirred. His head was aching and for a moment he had no idea where he was or what had happened. Eventually it all started coming back and he sat up abruptly, making his head ache even more.

'Damn,' he whispered, looking around. 'She's going to kill me . . . But why haven't the police come? He must have reported his kidnapping.'

The man took off his mask gingerly, his head hurting with every little touch. After taking off his gloves, he fiddled about in his pocket for his mobile phone. When he finally got it out, he looked at the time.

Two in the morning. He must have been out cold for hours.

His right leg hurt badly. He remembered falling on his knee on that blasted concrete during the fight. Then he noticed something else.

The gun, it's gone! Damn! Well at least I wore gloves so my fingerprints won't be on it . . . I've got to get out of this awful place before the cops come though.

He got up and limped slowly towards the stairs. Reaching them, he crawled up, his whole body aching, especially his head and his knee.

When he got to the door, he tried the knob, but the door wouldn't budge. He pushed it as hard as the pain would allow him, but nothing. He sat on the top step and took out his mobile again. Nervously, he dialled the number.

'Hi, um . . . I'm sorry but there's been a problem,' he said, not looking forward to his co-conspirator's response.

* * *

About half an hour later, David's kidnapper heard a key in the door. He was relieved, fearing that the police could arrive at any time. He was starting to feel claustrophobic as well and his head and leg still ached badly.

A woman stood at the door, not looking at all pleased with him.

'Well, I leave you to do the simplest of jobs and you muck it all up,' she said, glaring at him. 'Sometimes I think it would be better if I did everything myself. Not to mention that you woke me up in the middle of the night.'

'It would have been difficult for you to have pulled this off on your own.'

'We're not going to pull this off at all now, are we?' she growled. 'You've let all that money slip through your fingers. I chose an idiot to work with, I really did.'

'I don't think David recognised me, if that's any help. I didn't ever take the mask off.'

'He might have recognised your voice though. I think it's best if you leave the country.'

'I can't leave,' he said, incredulously.

'You can't expect me to just pack my bags and go.'

'David has probably gone to the police already and he may be able to identify you. You could well be arrested. Knowing you, you'll probably confess all and tell them about me. It's too great a risk.'

'I would never do that, hand you over to the police I mean.'

'You might do if you're frightened. How do I know that I can trust you?'

'But if I leave, they'll know it was me. I'll be the obvious suspect.'

'Well, there is one thing that may be in our favour. You said on the phone that David was ill. Hopefully, he's so ill that he can't tell the police anything yet. That will give us a little time. You do know that if you're caught and you blame me, I shall deny any knowledge of your crazy ideas.'

The man looked at her, wishing now that he hadn't been so eager to join forces with this woman, but it was a lot of money and he could certainly have done with it. Now however, that dream was all over.

'It's time you left,' she said abruptly. 'I'll see if I can find out anything and then we can make a final decision as to what we can do, though I still think you need to leave Crete . . . '

'Let's see what happens first,' he said.

As he left on his small motorbike, his head really hurt from putting his helmet on.

That woman is driving me mad, he thought as he drove along. *If she'd been more thoughtful, she would have come with me at David's meal times and stood guard at the top of the stairs, but she wanted me to do all the dirty work. Why on earth did I agree to do this?*

His bike then started spluttering and came to a stop. He had enough petrol; he was certain of that. He had put some in the previous day. All he wanted was to get home, have a bath and decide what to do next. Perhaps she was right. Perhaps he should go back to England, just in case David did know who was under that mask.

He parked up and decided to walk home. He'd sort the bike out later, but at the moment all he wanted to do was sleep. Damn that infernal leg though. It was getting more painful by the second.

11

Eve had decided to go to bed after all and at least try to get some sleep. However, after two hours she was still wide awake. When her phone rang, she was startled and wondered who could be ringing her at such a late hour. Could it be the kidnappers again? They hadn't changed their minds about giving her extra time to sort out her money, had they?

However, it wasn't them, but her friend Annie.

'Eve, I'm so worried. I've been sitting here for hours waiting for Pete, not knowing what to do. He went out for a jog earlier this evening and he hasn't come back. Do you think the kidnappers have him as well?'

'Oh,' Eve said, sounding surprised. 'I don't think so Annie. What would they expect to gain out of kidnapping him?'

'I don't know. Perhaps they were misinformed about our finances. Or perhaps he was involved in an accident. What do you think I should do?'

'Ring the police. Yes, that's the best thing.'

'What if they don't understand me? My Greek's not very good. And what if they say I've got to wait twenty four hours?'

'You'll have to insist that they do something. It is the middle of the night after all. He's hardly going to go somewhere at this time of night without telling you.'

'That's not what the police will think. They'll probably imagine he's having an affair. Perhaps I should go to the police station in Vamos. They'll find it more difficult to get rid of me if I'm there in person rather than on the end of a phone.'

'There might not be anyone there at night.'

'Well, I'll wait then.'

'Annie, don't you know where he goes jogging?'

'No. He goes all sorts of different places. He only started a few months ago. He said he was unfit and getting fat. He doesn't much like jogging; that's why he does different routes. It makes a change for him, you see.'

'Perhaps you should first go for a drive around the area to see if you can spot him, but you can't do that on your own. I'll come with you.'

'I can't ask you to do that.'

'Don't be silly, you're not asking. I'm offering. I can't sleep anyway. I'm just worrying about David, so it'll pass the time. You'll have to drive though as I was in The Black Cat this evening and had a few drinks. Give me ten minutes to get ready.'

Annie put the phone down with a sigh of relief. She felt a little guilty getting Eve out of bed, but she was glad to have the support of her friend.

* * *

David didn't know how long he'd slept, but he felt cold even though it was a warm night. His chest hurt and he still had a little difficulty breathing, but he knew he had to carry on. He had to get to safety before the kidnappers tracked him down.

David got up, feeling a bit shaky, but he found he could walk. He tried to keep as far away from the road as he could, staying in the olive groves as much as possible. He crouched down every time car lights passed. When one car stopped and then drove along slowly, he kept down for much longer.

About twenty minutes later, he felt tired again and decided to rest for a few minutes. However, he fell into a deep sleep and it was another two hours before he woke and managed to get up. This time when he started walking, a car illuminated a road sign and he was relieved. At last he knew where he was now and how he would be able to get to safety.

* * *

Annie drove slowly around all the villages in the area, Eve looking out of the windows. At one point, she thought she saw someone move and they stopped. However, whatever it was disappeared and they had to console themselves that it was probably a badger or beach marten.

At about three in the morning, they arrived at the police station in Vamos. To their huge disappointment, the door was locked. Annie burst into tears and Eve put her arms around her trying to console her.

'There, there, Annie. I'm sure someone will be here soon to open up early. We'll sit and wait in the car.'

'I can't ask you to stay, Eve. You have Robert to look after and you'll get no sleep,' she said, trying to stop sobbing. 'Not to mention all the worry with David.'

'If truth be told, Annie, I'm not sleeping well at all, so don't worry about me. Let's go back and sit in the car.'

Once there, they settled down and made sure both their mobile phones were on. Eve wished she'd prepared a flask of coffee.

The two women sat there in silence for a while and despite saying she wouldn't sleep much, all of a sudden Eve felt very tired and her eyes started to close. She was sure Annie wouldn't mind if she just had a little power nap.

The next thing Eve knew was Annie shaking her vigorously and talking excitedly.

'Eve wake up, Detective Chief Inspector Kastrinakis is going into the police station.'

'What?' Eve said sleepily. 'So early.'

'It's seven o'clock, Eve.'

'Oh, I'm so sorry. I dropped off.'

'You probably needed it. Shall we go in?'

'Yes, of course,' Eve said, but not before she grabbed her make-up bag and made sure she looked presentable.

Eve didn't like going anywhere without perfectly done make-up.

For once, Annie wasn't patient with Eve. Her husband could be lying half dead somewhere and Eve was putting on her lipstick.

'Oh, come on Eve, you look respectable enough. Can we just go in?' Annie said impatiently.

Eve decided she'd better leave her make-up as it was before Annie exploded.

Walking towards the police station Annie suddenly stopped.

'I'm scared, Eve, what if they've found Pete already and there are policemen knocking at my door right now?'

'Oh come now, Annie, I'm sure that isn't the case,' Eve said, trying to sound upbeat, but not really believing what she was saying. Anything was possible.

As they entered the police station, Dimitris Kastrinakis came out of his office to get a coffee. He stopped abruptly when he saw Eve and Annie.

Oh no, he thought. *Not Eve Masters again. What's brought her here at this time of the morning? She hasn't been doing anything stupid again trying to find David, has she?* he wondered.

Despite planning to be patient with her, Dimitris was finding it hard.

'Mrs Davies, Miss Masters, you are here early, what can I do for you?' he said, trying his hardest to be polite.

'My husband is missing,' Annie sobbed. 'He went out for a jog last night and he didn't come home. We drove around looking for him, but we had no luck.'

'I'm sorry, Mrs Davies,' the inspector said, thinking instead that the crimes surrounding the English community were getting out of hand.

'He could have been kidnapped,' Annie wailed. 'Or he could have fallen and hurt himself too badly to move, though why he hasn't phoned is beyond me.'

'Dimitris was stunned by this turn of events. He didn't think Annie and Pete had the sort of money Eve had, so why would anyone kidnap him? But of course he could have been killed by some mad drunkard who shouldn't have been driving, or simply fallen over and broken a bone.

'Did your husband have a mobile phone with him, Mrs Davies?'

'Yes, of course. I've tried dialling it over and over, but there's been no answer. Oh God, he could be dead for all we know.'

'Now, now, Mrs Davies, I know it's difficult, but try and stay positive. I take it you haven't telephoned the hospital?'

'No, my Greek's not good enough.'

'If you two go and sit in the hall for a little while, I will do some calling around.'

Annie and Eve did as they were told, but Annie felt even more despondent than before.

'He didn't give out much hope, did he?' Annie said to Eve, wiping away a few stray tears.

'What do you mean, Annie? He didn't say anything in particular. He's doing what he has to. He's phoning the hospital to see if Pete has been admitted and then I'm sure they'll start a search if he isn't there. What did you expect them to do?' she asked gently.

'Oh, I don't know. Promise me they'll find him. Reassure me. I don't know, Eve.'

All of a sudden, Annie burst into fresh floods of tears. She'd been trying to hold it in, but finally she was unable to any more. Eve put her arms around her, giving her a big hug.

'I'm sure they will find him, Annie. Hold on for a little longer.'

Annie got out a hanky and wiped away her tears, even though they were still flowing.

'Oh, Eve, I'm so selfish. You've been very kind, but you must be worried sick about David.'

'At least I know what I have to do to get him back. It's the uncertainty that's worse.'

Dimitris came out of his office and cleared his throat to get their attention. He could see that Annie was upset and he wanted to tread carefully.

Annie and Eve looked at Dimitris in anticipation.

'Your husband hasn't been admitted to the hospital in Chania, I'm afraid, so we'll have to organise a search. Do you know where he goes jogging, Mrs Davies?'

'No, he goes different-'

Annie was disturbed by a commotion at the front door of the police station. All of a sudden, Stavros came in with David hanging on to him.

Eve turned and couldn't believe her eyes. It was David! But what on earth had happened to him? He looked terrible, but at least he was free. However, Stavros was having difficulty holding him up and David suddenly slumped onto the concrete floor.

'David, darling,' she said rushing to him. 'Are you alright?'

Dimitris and the other officer lifted

David, who seemed to be out cold, and took him to a bench and laid him down. Much to Eve's relief, David's eyes started to flicker.

'What's happened to you my darling? Have you escaped from the kidnappers? You look so ill. Please, speak to me if you can.'

Dimitris sighed. So many questions, yet Eve could see that David was barely able to talk.

David coughed and although he was short of breath, he managed to say a few words.

'Eve, I . . . '

David seemed to drift off again, but Eve started to shake him.

'David! David, wake up! Oh, please wake up; don't die on me, please.'

'Calm down, Miss Masters,' Dimitris said coming over to them.

He looked at David and felt his pulse while Eve sat on the floor next to the bench sobbing.

'He's alive, Miss Masters, but he is obviously very ill. Stavros,' he called out to the other officer. 'Call for an ambulance.'

'Oh, David,' Eve sobbed. 'David . . . please . . . '

'Now, keep calm,' Dimitris said. 'He'll be in hospital soon and they can look after him there.'

Eve nodded as Stavros went to get a blanket. While he was gone, Dimitris tried to get David as comfortable as he could. However, as he moved him, the gun fell out of David's pocket.

'A gun!' Eve shrieked. 'It's not his, I swear. David doesn't own a gun . . . '

'Keep calm, Miss Masters, and don't touch it,' Dimitris snapped. 'If David escaped, it could be possible that he disarmed his kidnapper. Stavros,' he asked, as the junior officer came in with a blanket. 'Dust the gun for fingerprints.'

Eve went and sat near David, thinking it might be better if she were quiet. She knew she was getting worked-up, but she wanted to know everything straight away.

Eve got up and sat on the bench next to David. She took his hand and his eyes flickered open. She thought she could see the glimmer of a smile.

Please let him recover, please, Eve prayed, resolving to go to church more often if David got better. She was a Catholic, but only went to church now and again, her excuse being that the nearest Roman Catholic Church was in Chania and a little far to go on a Sunday morning. However, the distance didn't stop her going into Chania for dinner or to shop whenever she felt like it.

Annie hovered, not knowing what to do. Yes, she was worried about David, but the police officers seemed to have forgotten about Pete. They were more intent on waiting for the ambulance.

'Chief Inspector,' she finally said. 'What about my husband?'

'Ah yes, your husband. Yes, we must arrange the search as soon as possible. However, Mr Baker's escape puts a different light on his disappearance, doesn't it?'

'What do you mean?' Annie asked, suddenly feeling scared.

'Well, David has escaped from his kidnappers. Perhaps he had to fight with one of them to get away. Your husband is missing, Mrs Davies. There is a chance that he could be involved.'

'No, he can't be,' Annie cried out, bursting into tears again.

Eve was speechless for once. How could Dimitris think that their friend Pete had anything to do with this?

No, it can't be true . . . I refuse to believe it. Pete and David are friends. If he and Annie were desperate for money, they would ask us for a loan; I'm sure of it. There's no way Annie has any knowledge of a kidnapping; she's worried sick about her husband. Oh David, you have to wake up soon and tell us what's happened.

12

Eve sat outside the emergency room at Chania hospital waiting for the doctor to finish examining David. Every couple of minutes she got up and paced along the corridor, occasionally looking inside the ER to see if she could go in to be with him. However, the doctor was still checking him over.

'Miss Masters,' Dimitris finally exclaimed, a little weary of her eternal pacing. 'Why don't you sit down and wait for the doctor to come out. I'm sure you'll be told what's wrong with him as soon as he knows himself.'

'I can't just sit down and wait. David is very sick and I would have thought they'd know what's wrong with him by now. We've been here for ages. How would you feel in my position, Detective Chief Inspector Kastrinakis? I'm sure you wouldn't be sitting around waiting patiently.'

Dimitris sighed. The old Eve was emerging, but he did understand how worried she must be. He would be as well if it was his wife. Anyway, he was also keen for the doctor to finish the examination. Dimitris wanted to question David and hopefully apprehend the kidnapper as soon as possible.

Annie was very quiet. She had wanted to go with the police to search for her husband, but Dimitris wouldn't let her. He said it was best that she went home and waited for news, but she wasn't having any of that. If she wasn't allowed to go on the search, she would accompany Eve to the hospital. Eve needed a friend with her for starters and hopefully David would wake up soon and Pete would be exonerated.

There is absolutely no way Pete is the kidnapper, she thought. *How can the police even think that? He's a good man. We're not that short of money that he has to resort to kidnapping a friend of ours. I hope that Eve doesn't believe it.*

'I wish the doctors would tell us something,' Eve said, plonking herself down next to Annie.

Annie was miles away and barely heard Eve.

'Annie, are you alright?'

'Yes, I'm . . . '

Annie stopped, feeling tears starting to fall once again.

'Oh Annie, take no notice of what the police have said,' Eve whispered so that Dimitris didn't hear her. 'I haven't any doubts that Pete is completely innocent.'

Annie forced a smile. However, the alternative was probably not good news either. If Pete wasn't the kidnapper, he could be lying hurt somewhere. Perhaps somebody attacked him and stole his mobile phone which was why he hadn't rung her. He could even be dead.

David's doctor came out of the emergency room at last and Eve jumped up.

'Is there any news, doctor?'

'Yes. Mr Baker has pneumonia and will have to be admitted for treatment and observation.'

'Is . . . is he going to be alright?'

'He seems to be a fit man so I have high hopes that he will recover.'

'We need to speak to him as soon as possible,' Dimitris said before Eve could say anything else.

'I'm afraid that won't be possible at the moment, Chief Inspector.'

'Why?' Eve butted in. 'What's wrong?'

'He did wake up, but he's having trouble staying awake and it's better he rests. Also, he is finding it very difficult to talk as he's so short of breath.'

'This is an important police matter. I only have a couple of questions to ask. I won't be long,' Dimitris spoke again.

'Very well, you can go in for a few minutes, but no longer. He will be moved to a ward soon and needs rest and also oxygen at regular intervals.'

Dimitris thanked the doctor and

walked into the ward, followed closely by Eve.

'I don't think you were given permission to come in, Miss Masters.'

'I have to see David, if only for five minutes.'

Dimitris said no more, knowing he would do the same if it was his wife in there.

As they went into the emergency room, Eve felt herself shiver. She didn't really know why. Both times she had been poisoned, she had passed out and had woken up in a ward, but she imagined that she must first have come into ER.

Eve suddenly felt guilty. It was all her fault that David was here. If she wasn't his girlfriend, he wouldn't have been kidnapped and ended up in hospital. Perhaps when he got better he might think the same thing and end their relationship. He might think she was too much of a liability.

Eve looked over to the man she loved. Despite his tan he looked pale.

He was hooked up to an oxygen mask and seemed to be asleep.

Eve rushed past Dimitris and went to David. She took his hand and started talking before Dimitris could say a word.

'David, I'm so sorry. If you hadn't have met me, you wouldn't be in this position. I wouldn't blame you if you called the wedding off.'

Dimitris stood by, listening. For once he actually felt a little sorry for Eve. It wasn't really her fault, but he could understand her blaming herself.

David then pressed Eve's hand and tried to take off his oxygen mask, but he seemed too weak. Dimitris went to help, knowing he had to keep it brief.

'I know you're ill, but can you answer one question?' Dimitris asked. 'Was it Mr Davies who kidnapped you?'

David seemed to frown, but as he tried to say something, he started wheezing and was out of breath. He couldn't say a word. A nurse rushed over to put the mask back on and had a few angry words with Dimitris.

'I presume you will be staying here with your fiancé, Miss Masters?' Dimitris asked Eve.

'Of course, where else would I go?' she snapped, looking at the officer intently.

Dimitris ignored her attitude for once, knowing she was upset.

'Well, I must join the search for Mr Davies. Could you phone me if David says anything?'

'Yes, of course,' Eve replied a little guiltily, knowing she had been sharp. It was important after all that they found out the name of the kidnapper as soon as possible.

'Will you keep Mrs Davies here with you? We have her number and will phone as soon as we find anything relating to her husband.'

'Yes I will. I don't think she should be driving on her own anyway,' Eve replied. 'She hasn't slept all night.'

Eve wished Dimitris would leave so she could concentrate on David.

However, as soon as he had left, she heard a commotion at the other end of the emergency room.

'Be careful,' a loud voice boomed. 'If my hip wasn't broken, it certainly is now.'

Eve groaned inside. What were the odds of finding Betty in hospital at the same time as David? To make matters worse, they wheeled her to a bed which was only two away from his. Eve had no option but to go over and talk to her.

'Betty, what a surprise seeing you here. What's happened to you?'

'Eve, can I never get away from you?' Betty snapped. 'If you're really interested, I fell down the stairs and believe my hip could be broken; well I'm sure it is broken now after the rough handling I've had.'

'Oh dear, I'm so sorry,' Eve said, trying to sound as sympathetic as possible.

Betty wasn't fooled though.

'You don't care what happens to me. You're probably laughing your socks off.'

'That's a harsh thing to say, Betty. Of course I'm sorry you've had an accident.'

'Humph,' was all Betty could say.

'Where's Don? Is he not with you?' Eve asked naughtily, knowing he was staying in a hotel as he and Betty had split up.

'He's . . . he's not well himself. I told him to stay in bed today.'

'Oh, really? He seemed absolutely fine at The Black Cat last night. We were sorry to miss you.'

Betty looked dumbfounded and was just gathering her thoughts to give a clever retort when Eve's mobile rang. Seeing it was Robert, she answered it, moving away towards David.

'I've just got up and found your note. Are you and Annie still looking for Pete? You must be completely shattered.'

'Robert, so much has happened since I left. Oh, dear . . . ' Eve burst into tears.

'Calm down Eve. Tell me exactly

what's happened since I went to bed last night.'

Eve wiped away her tears and then started to recount the events of the night.

'And now I'm at the hospital. David's got pneumonia and hasn't yet been able to tell us who kidnapped him. The police even think it might be Pete as he's missing. David could have fought with him and now he's lying somewhere and we don't know where.'

'Calm down, Eve, I'm pretty sure it isn't Pete. He seems such a nice guy. I expect Annie's in a bit of a state?'

'That's an understatement. Poor woman. She's been frantic all night worrying that something awful has happened to Pete and now that the police have suggested that he might have kidnapped David, she's in a terrible state. Personally, I don't believe it,' Eve whispered down the phone.

'Why are you talking so quietly, Eve. I can barely hear you.'

'Betty's just come in. It looks like

she's broken a hip.'

'Is Don with her?'

'No. Actually, I feel a bit guilty. I was teasing her a bit about where Don was.'

'You should go and apologise, Eve. She's probably upset.'

'Well, she lied about Don, making out they were still together.'

'Eve, go and apologise,' Robert said sternly.

'No, I won't apologise,' Eve replied stubbornly. 'However, I will go and see if she needs anything.'

'Good. Do you want me to come to the hospital, Eve? Do you need anything?'

'No, I'm OK. I came in Annie's car and I think I'll drive her home later. She wasn't driving very steadily and it's best she has company.'

'I'll wait to hear from you then, Eve.'

She put her mobile into her bag and moved closer to David and took his hand.

'I'll find out who did this to you, I promise.'

Then Eve remembered about Betty and turned to look at her. She was arguing with a doctor and Eve smiled. That woman would never change.

Once the doctor had gone, she heard Betty shout over to her.

'Is that David there? What's wrong with him?'

Eve got up and walked over to Betty, not wanting to shout over the Greek family surrounding the bed next to David's.

'He has pneumonia, Betty.'

Eve decided not to elaborate. She didn't want to tell her the whole story of David's kidnapping and Pete's disappearance. Perhaps Betty knew something already anyway. News travelled fast around the villages, even when you were completely certain there was no way the information could have got out.

Betty, however, didn't seem to know anything and seemed genuinely sorry.

'Oh, how terrible,' she remarked. 'I hope he recovers soon.'

'Thanks,' Eve said, now feeling even guiltier about her attitude to Betty earlier on. Still, that woman usually gave as good as she got and recently she had been even more unpleasant.

'He's a bit out of it at the moment, but I'll give him your regards.'

Betty nodded and Eve excused herself quickly, not feeling comfortable when talking normally with Betty. She had completely forgotten to ask Betty if she needed anything.

Eve walked out into the corridor to tell Annie about Betty.

'Does she know anything?' Annie asked nervously, keeping her voice down.

'I don't think so and all I said was that David had pneumonia. She seemed truly surprised. I didn't mention Pete at all.'

'Thank you, Eve. I couldn't bear it if rumours about Pete being a kidnapper started spreading; I really couldn't.'

Annie looked close to tears again and Eve gave her a hug.

'Well, you'd better cheer up then as I doubt Betty would believe you were this upset about David being ill.'

Annie attempted a smile and they sat there in silence for a few minutes. Suddenly the doors opened and David was wheeled out in his bed by some orderlies. Eve leapt up, grabbing Annie and they followed. She expected he was being taken to a ward and she was right.

Once upstairs and settled, Eve asked Annie what she wanted to do now. Eve wanted to stay with David, but Annie couldn't drive home in the state she was in.

'I don't know. I keep looking at my phone hoping the police will ring with some good news, but they haven't. Oh, where is he, Eve? Where is my husband?'

Eve didn't know what to say, but in the end thought it best to get Annie home. Annie had barely slept the previous night and needed to get some rest and Eve had to get some things for

David's hospital stay. However, she didn't want to leave him; he looked so vulnerable lying there asleep. Still it was better he rested and she could be back in a couple of hours anyway.

'Come on, Annie, I think you need to get home.'

* * *

Annie fell asleep on the journey home. She was so tired after being up all night and had virtually used up all her energy crying. Eve glanced over at her and hoped against hope that Pete wasn't involved in David's disappearance. It would destroy Annie's world. And what if Pete was involved with another woman and they planned to run away after they got the money? What if it was that appalling woman, Joanna? It didn't bear thinking about.

Eve remembered the murders earlier in the summer when she had seen Pete with Lucy Fowler, one of the two murder victims, in Rethymnon. She had vaguely suspected him of having an affair with Lucy, although she really couldn't believe it.

But what if he had? It's not altogether impossible. He didn't murder her, but he could still have had an affair. Oh dear, she must get these thoughts out of her head and try to stay positive for Annie.

It wasn't long before they arrived at Eve's house. With Annie fast asleep, Eve had put her foot down and had probably gone way over the speed limit a few too many times, but she wanted to get back to the hospital as soon as she could.

As they parked up, Annie suddenly woke up and Eve caught a smidgeon of fear in her eyes.

'It's OK Annie, we're at my house. We'll get a coffee and something to eat and I'll see what Robert's up to.'

'I don't think I could eat.'

'You must try, Annie. You're looking exhausted and you do need something to keep you going.'

Annie nodded as Robert came out of the front door with Portia at his heel. The dog was wagging her tail, hopeful for a walk, but she was going to have to wait.

'Hello, you two. I wasn't expecting you back so soon,' Robert said.

Eve explained her decision to come back, and then ushered Annie into the house. She got her comfortable in the lounge before going into the kitchen to start making breakfast.

'I honestly don't know how much more Annie can take. She's exhausted and she's so worried about Pete.'

'And what about you, Eve?'

'I'm fine.'

'Don't give me that. You're pretending to be fine for Annie's sake, aren't you?'

'Don't make me collapse into a heap, Robert. I'm using all my energy to keep on top of this. Somebody has to for Annie's sake. At least David has escaped . . . but he's ill, Robert, very ill.'

Eve felt a lump in her throat, but instead of bursting into tears, she shook her head and moved away to start breakfast.

'It doesn't matter if you cry, Eve. I won't think any less of you.'

Eve smiled. 'I've already had my fair share of tears. Now it's time to move on and find out who the kidnapper is. I also need to be there for Annie; just in case . . . '

Eve's voice trailed away.

'You're right,' Robert agreed. 'This situation is far from over.'

Eve started breakfast, while Robert got the coffee on.

'Have you told Don about Betty yet?' Robert asked Eve.

'Why should I?' she asked. 'He's washed his hands of her. Why stir things up?'

'Eve, that's very callous. She's probably scared and will need help in hospital, particularly if she can't walk. You know the nursing staff don't do nearly as much in the hospitals here as they do in England.'

Eve knew Robert was right and she should help, but she was finding it hard to be kind to Betty. After all, that woman was rude and nasty to her all the time.

'OK, I'll ring him after breakfast,' she reluctantly agreed. 'Then he can make his own mind up.'

'Oh, by the way, Alison's on her way. She's managed to wangle a few days' leave. She's having to fly Aegean so has to change in Athens and won't be here until late evening. I suppose I'd better hire a car as you might need yours.'

Eve got the impression that Robert wasn't happy about hiring a car. Although he'd lent her the money she needed, when it came to everyday things, Robert was always on the lookout for a bargain. She remembered his first trip to Crete the previous summer when he'd been quite happy for Eve to pay for all the meals out and for her to drive him around. When he'd come over at Christmas with Alison, he did hire a car, but Eve thought it was probably Alison's influence that made him do it.

'Yes, it probably is best if you hire a car,' Eve said. 'You'll probably end up doing things for Betty once she sees Alison is here.'

'I'm supposed to be here to give you help and support, not Betty!'

'And you will I'm sure. In fact you can look after Annie while I go back to the hospital.'

Robert shrugged his shoulders. It seemed to him he was being given all the menial jobs to do. However, he then remembered being in Eve's car when the brakes hadn't worked. They had almost been killed and he didn't really want anything like that to happen again.

It wasn't long before breakfast was ready and Eve went to wake Annie up.

'Oh my goodness, have I been asleep? I was so sure I wouldn't drop off.'

'You obviously needed it. Come on, Annie, I've made breakfast.'

Annie was confronted with a plate of sausages, bacon, eggs, mushroom and beans.

'I don't know if I can do this justice, Eve.'

'Just try and eat a little,' Eve replied, glancing towards Robert who was making short work of his breakfast.

Eve suddenly felt hungry herself, hardly having eaten much since David had been kidnapped. She needed to start practising what she preached and she started on her vegetarian sausages, soon beginning to feel a little less light headed as she ate. She had felt quite faint at the hospital, but had tried to ignore the feeling and push past it, not wanting to be admitted into hospital herself. Twice was quite enough for her.

Annie started to pick her way through her breakfast, not wanting Eve's work to all be for nothing, but she was forcing it down.

'Oh, why don't the police call?' she asked. 'They should have found Pete by now.'

'They have a big area to cover, Annie,' Eve replied. 'They haven't been looking for long, but I'm sure they'll phone as soon as they find him.'

Annie nodded, but neither she, Eve nor Robert were convinced of anything any more.

* * *

While Annie was having a rest after breakfast, Eve picked up the phone ready to ring Don. She still didn't want to, believing that he was much better off without Betty, but she did realise that he had to be told. Eve was simply worried that he might return to Betty out of duty.

Don answered after a couple of rings.

'Eve, how nice to hear from you. I had a lovely evening in The Black Cat last night. I can't tell you how pleasant it was to chat without being reprimanded for the things I say.'

'Yes, it was a very pleasant evening, but today isn't so good, I'm afraid.'

Perhaps she should only tell him about David having pneumonia.

'What's wrong Eve?' Don asked. He was eager to help if he could. She had been such a good friend.

'Oh, David's in hospital with pneumonia and . . . '

'Oh, how terrible for you,' he interrupted. 'I hope he gets better soon. Luckily, he is a fit man.'

Eve paused, knowing she had to go through with it.

'While I was in ER, Betty came in.'

'Betty? Was she with someone who was sick?'

'No, she fell down the stairs and hurt her hip. It could be broken.'

'Fell where?'

'Down the last few stairs at your house,' Eve replied, surprised that he hadn't asked how she was. Perhaps Don really didn't care about her after all.

'She's done that a few times. I knew she'd break something eventually.'

Eve didn't know what to say to that.

'I suppose I should go to the hospital and see if she needs some help.'

'Yes, it's not easy in the hospital with so few nursing staff.'

'It doesn't change anything, Eve; I'm not going to rush back to her if that's what you think.'

'You must do what's right for you,' Eve stated.

However, she was glad that he hadn't decided to go back to Betty. Of course that could all change in the next few days.

'Oh, by the way, Don, Alison's coming over today, so I'm sure that will help with Betty's care.'

'Yes, yes it will. Is Robert picking her up?'

'Yes, he is.'

'OK. I'd better be off to the hospital then.'

Eve said her goodbyes, knowing that it was time for her to return to the hospital as well.

* * *

Robert took Annie to the local shop after Eve had gone. Annie had tried to sleep, but although she had managed to in the car, her mind was too active now. She thought it might be better to try and keep busy. Eve had asked her if she wanted to go home, but she'd said she'd rather not be alone. Eve hoped Robert didn't mind.

Once in the shop, Annie took ages doing the little shopping she needed. She spent quite a while looking at packets and trying to understand the Greek. She hoped that it might take her mind off Pete.

Robert was bored with wandering around the shop, so he started chatting to Stamatis, the owner of the shop. Stamatis spoke very good English which was a great bonus for the holidaymakers when they came in.

His shop was a treasure trove and fulfilled practically every need. Stamatis had a big storeroom at the back as well. He was very clever; putting to the front of the shop whatever might sell on a particular day. If it was raining, out came the umbrellas and Macs, if it was hot, he brought out the fans, lilos and buckets and spades. He never missed an opportunity, especially as he opened at seven in the morning and didn't shut until eleven at night, keeping much longer hours than any other shop in the area.

Robert had met him on his previous visits and they had talked about politics, religion and football and today was no exception. Robert enjoyed the chats, finding it interesting to learn more about Greek life and culture. In the end he hardly knew how long Annie had spent doing her shopping.

'Ah, Mr Robert,' Stamatis said, making Robert smile at the addition of 'Mr' in front of his Christian name. It seemed quite common for Greeks to call English people with their title and first name. 'Here is my niece come to cover my shop while I go to the hospital.'

'Oh, I'm sorry, are you ill or is it a

member of the family?'

'It is my grandmother. She has had a stroke I'm afraid. She is ninety so these things will happen.'

'I hope she recovers,' Robert said. 'I have a friend in hospital, David, David Baker.'

'Oh no, what is wrong with Mr David. He is a good customer and friend of mine.'

Robert smiled to himself again, thinking that anyone who spent money in his shop was a friend!

'He has pneumonia.'

'Oh, that is not so good. I will visit him later.'

With that, Stamatis took his leave, leaving Robert wondering if he should have told him more about David.

13

Dimitris Kastrinakis had already paired Stavros with a junior officer and told them to start searching for Pete Davies. Once he had left the hospital, he started an additional search together with another junior officer.

Dimitris and Stavros had planned which villages and surrounding areas each pair would go to, but Dimitris wasn't happy. It was a scorching hot and unusually humid day, the heat on Crete normally being dry. He knew they'd get hot, sticky and uncomfortable.

Dimitris wondered if Pete really was the kidnapper. He didn't know the man well, but he thought him polite and unobtrusive. Pete had even made the effort to learn Greek which many ex-pats hadn't bothered to do.

He pondered on all the possibilities.

If Pete wasn't the kidnapper, he was probably lying injured somewhere and it could take hours to find him. If he was the kidnapper, David could have fought with him and locked him up in the place where he had been kept. They would never find that without David's help. Of course, if David hadn't managed to lock him in, he may have even left the island. There were so many possibilities; if only David Baker would wake up and talk.

A couple of hours later, having had no luck in their searches, Dimitris and Stavros and their men met up to take a short break and decide where else to look.

Dimitris cursed the austerity measures. If it wasn't for all the cut backs, he might have had more officers to help search for Mr Davies. Perhaps he could even have been given police dogs. As it was, there were four policeman searching acre upon acre of land.

* * *

An hour and a half later, the police were still searching for Pete Davies, Dimitris thinking that if they didn't find him, it was highly likely that he was the kidnapper and had made himself scarce. Dimitris felt a great deal of sympathy for Annie. He didn't think she was involved; if she was, she was a damn good actress.

Dimitris thought back to the time before Eve had arrived on the island. Life seemed simpler then. Now it was one drama after another.

His thoughts were interrupted by shouting in the distance. He called his junior officer over and they both walked quickly towards the noise. As they got nearer, Dimitris was certain somebody was calling for help. Soon both officers could see a man sitting on the ground, waving.

'It's him,' Dimitris cried. 'It's Pete Davies.'

Both men ran towards him.

'My goodness, I'm glad you two have found me,' Pete said, thankfully. I didn't think anyone would come. I can't walk particularly well; I think it's my knee.'

'Why didn't you phone for help?' Dimitris asked suspiciously.

'I went to use my mobile and it was dead. Annie must be worried sick.'

'Yes she is, very worried. I'm afraid, however, that we have some questions to ask you, but they can wait until you're in hospital. Kostas, phone for an ambulance,' he instructed the other man.

'Questions? What questions?'

'Very well, we've reason to believe that you may be involved in the kidnapping of David Baker.'

Pete's face fell.

'I didn't even know he'd been kidnapped.'

He couldn't believe it. He had been a policeman, a law abiding citizen, and here he was being accused of kidnapping!

Pete tried to get up. He wanted to get the interview done as soon as possible, but Dimitris had moved away to make some phone calls and he'd have to wait. He'd also have to stop himself from falling apart. The thought of jail in a foreign country scared him — and Annie, what must she be going through?

Soon, the ambulance came and Pete was taken to the hospital, followed by Dimitris and Kostas.

Dimitris hoped that David Baker had improved and could give them a statement. One thing Dimitris hated was questioning other police officers. However, he had no choice. Pete Davies was his only suspect at the moment.

* * *

Before they left, Dimitris had telephoned Annie, telling her that Pete was safe, but was being taken to the hospital. He had also told her that he would meet her there.

On the one hand, Annie was relieved that Pete was safe, even though he had been injured, but on the other hand, she started to panic when Dimitris said he would meet her at the hospital. Did this mean that the police really suspected him of kidnapping David?

Robert had brought Annie home from the shop a little while before the phone call and they had just sat in front of the television. Annie needed to be distracted and TV seemed to be the best thing. However, after the phone call from Dimitris, Annie became frantic.

'I have to go to the hospital immediately, Robert. The police have found Pete and he's been injured. I know they suspect him of kidnapping, but I know he didn't. He's a good man. He would never do anything like that to a friend of his.'

'I'm sure he wouldn't Annie,' Robert replied.

He looked at her and all he saw was a quivering mess. He knew he couldn't let her drive in the state she was in.

'Calm down Annie,' he said gently.

'You don't know what's going on. However, I think I should drive you to the hospital.'

'If you're sure, Robert,' she replied, knowing that this was the best plan.

'Good. Let's get ready.'

Annie tried to smile, but all she kept thinking about was how her husband, a reputable and fair police officer, would cope in prison.

* * *

In the hospital, Pete was waiting to see a doctor. He wished one would hurry up as the pain in his knee was getting worse and he could certainly do with some painkillers.

He was also keen to get his interview with the police over and done with.

'Mr Davies,' Dimitris said, coming over to Pete. 'The doctor seems to be taking a long time so I may as well ask my questions now.'

'Please do,' Pete replied, hoping his innocence would shine through as he replied to the questions.

'So, Mr Davies, can you tell me what were you doing yesterday evening?'

'I went jogging at about half past eight. I was passing through an olive grove when I fell and hurt my leg, my knee in fact. I didn't think I'd make it much further so I stayed put, hoping that someone would rescue me.'

'Didn't you have your mobile with you?'

'Yes, but when I tried to ring Annie, I found out that the battery was dead.'

'So you stayed in the place where we found you all night?'

'Yes. I did not kidnap David and I have no idea why you're accusing me.'

'You were missing when Mr Baker escaped from his kidnappers, so we have to ask questions. Of course, when David wakes up, he should be able to tell us who did kidnap him. That will clear everything up.'

'That is, if he knows whoever it was.'

Dimitris studied Pete. He didn't think he was the kidnapper, but you never knew what people might end up doing, especially for money.

Dimitris decided to leave Kostas with Pete and he went to check on David's condition. Hopefully there had been a change.

Arriving at the ward, he saw Eve sitting by David's bed, looking very solemn.

'Miss Masters, any change?' he asked.

'Not really,' she replied. 'David seems to be sleeping far too much. What do you think? He did wake up for a little while and I asked him who the kidnapper was, but he seemed to have no idea what I was talking about. He did remember me, thank goodness, but whatever happened in the last couple of days seems to have deserted him. I'm really worried.'

'Keep calm. I'm sure he'll remember more when he's better.'

'Robert, my friend, has called to say you've found Pete. He's not admitted to the kidnap, has he?' she asked anxiously.

'No, he's adamant that he wasn't involved.'

'But you don't believe him?'

'I am open-minded. It would be best if David woke up. Then we could be sure.'

Eve nodded, but she was very concerned. What would it do to Annie if Pete was guilty?

* * *

Annie couldn't sit still in the car driving to the hospital. She fidgeted and kept wringing her hands. Robert was worried about her so he put his foot on the accelerator. The sooner he got to the hospital and she was reunited with her husband, the better.

As soon as they arrived, Annie jumped out of the car and dashed in, Robert having great difficulty in keeping up with her. Entering the hospital, she stopped, not knowing where to go, and then she burst into tears.

'Hey, calm down Annie, we're here

now,' Robert said gently, a little out of breath from running after her.

'Where do we go? I don't know what to do,' Annie sobbed.

Robert suggested going to ER and once there, Annie saw Pete who was still waiting to be seen by a doctor.

'Oh Pete,' Annie screamed as soon as she saw him. 'I thought I'd lost you.'

'Hey,' he said pulling her close. 'I've only hurt my knee, possibly broken it. I'll be fine.'

'But the police . . . '

'I know, Annie, I know they suspect me of kidnapping David, but I swear to you that I didn't. You do believe me, don't you darling?'

'Of course I do,' Annie replied, hugging him tightly again.

14

Eve was dozing by the side of David's bed when she felt someone shake her. She looked up to see Robert and attempted to smile.

'Annie's with Pete now,' he said. 'He's broken his knee and I believe they're going to put titanium plates in it.'

'I'm sure Annie will be relieved to have him back safe and almost sound.'

'She would be if the police weren't considering him a suspect in David's kidnapping.'

'Oh, what nonsense. Pete would never kidnap David. After all, they've been friends for years. I can't believe that the police have actually accused him of it.'

After worrying how Annie would cope if Pete were guilty, Eve had decided how silly she was being. How could he be one of the kidnappers? His friendship with David was far too strong for such a betrayal.

Robert, meanwhile, was looking at David.

'Has he been asleep for long, Eve?'

'Most of the time, apart from a couple of wheezing fits.'

'I'm sure he'll be alright,' Robert said. 'He's as tough as old boots.'

Eve attempted to smile again, but then her face became angry. She was looking behind Robert and when he turned around, he saw Joanna and Kevin entering the ward.

'What are you doing here?' Eve asked sharply, looking at Joanna.

However, it was Kevin who answered.

'David's a friend and I wanted to see how he was. We were in the local shop and heard that David was here.'

Eve softened a little. After all, David and Kevin did get on well. Plus Kevin had been through a difficult time lately, what with his wife being murdered and his brother ending up in prison. But why did that infernal woman have to come as well?

Eve decided that her best course of action was to speak to Kevin and ignore Joanna.

'Yes, Kevin,' she said emphasising his name. 'David's in a bad way, but they're doing everything they can. He's had trouble speaking, but hopefully that will change now he's having regular bursts of oxygen.'

Joanna, who never liked being ignored, spoke even before Kevin had a chance to say anything.

'Well I hope this dispels any ideas that we're the kidnappers.'

'I didn't ever think Kevin was capable of doing something so awful.'

Robert could see that Joanna was about to say something so he interrupted quickly.

'Well I must say, this has been a strange day. So many ex-pats admitted to hospital, one after the other.'

Kevin, also hoping that there wouldn't be another confrontation, jumped in.

'Who else is here?'

'Well, Pete's broken his knee and then there's Betty. She fell down a few stairs and it seems like she's broken a hip.'

'My goodness,' Kevin laughed, trying to lighten the mood. 'I think everyone who wants to visit will be able to carpool — it'll save a lot of money in petrol.'

Eve and Robert both grinned, but then Eve became more serious.

'I'm not going to leave the hospital. After all, the kidnappers might turn up and try to kill David.'

'Oh, what nonsense,' Joanna said. 'They've probably left the country already.'

Eve thought Joanna was trying, in some feeble sort of way, to show that she wasn't one of the kidnappers. She was as bold as brass and was probably attempting to fool them all. Eve still believed that Joanna was behind the plot to kidnap David and she was going to prove it.

* * *

Pete Davies was sitting up in his hospital bed. He was a little fed up after hearing that he had a broken kneecap and was facing a long hospital stay. However, it wasn't all bad. At least the police couldn't throw him in jail for the moment.

Annie sat by his side, still feeling confused as well as concerned for her husband. She was usually a strong woman, but she seemed unable to calm down. She was certain that the police would soon be back again to question Pete and that there would be no way for him to prove that he wasn't one of the kidnappers.

'Cheer up, Annie; I'll be as good as new in no time at all.'

However, Annie wasn't up to being cheerful.

'What if the police arrest you? They might not find the real kidnappers and decide the only person to have committed the crime is you. They'll probably want to look at our bank books to see how much money we have, or don't have. We struggle through each month, don't we darling?'

'That doesn't make us kidnappers, Annie. They have no proof,' Pete said, trying to convince Annie that everything would be alright.

However, he didn't tell Annie that the same things had crossed his mind as well, just as Annie didn't dare share her next thought with Pete.

What if they charge you anyway because there's no-one else to arrest? It didn't bear thinking about.

* * *

Betty couldn't believe that Don had come to see her, thinking he must have an ulterior motive.

'So why have you come, Don? I believe we'd said everything that needed to be said when you left our home.'

'I thought you might need some help.'

'I can manage very well on my own, thank you. You've made it clear that you don't want to be with me, so there's no point being nice now.'

'I still care for you, Betty,' he admitted. 'But-'

'But you don't care enough to stay married to me. I know that's what you're going to say.'

Don said nothing. Yes, he felt sorry for her and yes, he probably did still love her a little or perhaps the memory of her when they were younger. He thought it must be atrociously painful to have a broken hip, but he'd made the break from her now and if he put her under the illusion that he was coming back to her, he'd never forgive himself.

He deserved to be able to do what he wanted and be happy. Unfortunately, Betty had been making him completely miserable for a very long time now.

* * *

Eve wished Joanna and Kevin would leave. She understood why Kevin was there, but wondered why he'd had to bring that unpleasant and nosey woman with him.

It was obvious that the two women didn't like each other and it was hardly the right time for Joanna to rile Eve. However, Kevin didn't seem to realise that he had acted foolishly.

Robert eventually told Eve he was going to see Annie, hoping that would spark Joanna and Kevin to leave. He could see how fed up Eve was becoming having Joanna in such close proximity.

Eve was very tired but she was determined not to sleep. Instead she let her mind wander and ignored the other visitors by the bed.

It wasn't long before her thoughts were disturbed by a rough voice saying her name. She looked up and David was awake, looking a little bit brighter.

'David, you've woken up at last,' she said with a definite sigh of relief. 'Oh darling, I was so worried about you.'

Eve bent over to give David a gentle hug so as not to hurt his already weary body.

Joanna and Kevin were still there, seemingly unaware that they'd outstayed their welcome

'You'll now be able to tell us who kidnapped you,' Eve continued. 'The police think it was Pete, but I'm sure it wasn't. You and he are such good friends. Once you've told Dimitris who the kidnappers are, he can go and arrest them,' Eve added looking pointedly at Joanna. 'You can just relax and get better without worrying about anything. To think, they thought they could get that much money out of me. I would have paid it of course. I love you so much. Luckily they haven't got away with it. They didn't reckon on you escaping, did they?'

Eve finally stopped talking. She had so much to tell David, but it was difficult to get it all out at once. However, his reaction wasn't at all as she had hoped. He looked at Eve quizzically before speaking in a whisper.

'Kidnapped,' he rasped. 'Was I kidnapped? When did this happen? The last thing I remember was saying goodbye to you in the morning. I take it that wasn't this morning, was it?'

Eve looked at David in despair. How could he have forgotten?

'I really am sorry Eve, but I can't remember being kidnapped, or escaping, or anything.'

Eve glanced at Joanna and was sure she could see a faint smile on her face.

* * *

Dimitris Kastrinakis was fed up. He had thought that he would be able to close the case very quickly, but that was now a forgotten hope. David remembered nothing, but this could change at any time. He was still in danger and the kidnappers could have gone into hiding with a plan to get to David in the hospital. For all Dimitris knew, they could be plotting to kill him now.

And what if Pete Davies is one of them? He's right here in the hospital and he's a clever man. Yes, he has a broken knee, but he could persuade his wife to do something to David. What if she was in it from the beginning?

'Miss Masters,' Dimitris said, taking Eve to one side. 'I haven't really got the resources, but I'm going to get a police officer to stand guard outside Mr Baker's ward.'

'What?' Eve asked. 'You think the kidnappers are going to come and kill David, don't you?'

She couldn't believe that there were even more things to worry about.

'I don't know if they'll try anything, but it's best to be safe. There's a good chance he'll get his memory back and be able to identify them. Anyway, you look tired. Go home and rest. You can't stay here day and night.'

Eve nodded. She had to lend her car to Robert to pick up Alison from the airport anyway and she was very tired.

However, would she be able to sleep knowing that David could still be in danger? This was turning into a nightmare. It had been fun solving the previous cases, but this was far too personal. At the moment she just wanted to pack her bags, grab David and get on the first plane back to England.

15

Eve, to her surprise, slept well, although she did wake up earlier than normal. She felt a little guilty for sleeping so soundly while David was in hospital and in pain, but realised that the lack of sleep she had endured during the previous couple of days must have caught up with her.

In the daylight, things didn't seem half as bad as they had done the previous night. David was being guarded so he should be safe while he was in the hospital. While he was there the kidnappers wouldn't be able to get to him, but what would happen when he left?

Hopefully he would get his memory back before he was sent home and the kidnappers could be put behind bars.

Eve took her coffee outside and sat there with Portia. The sun was already powerful at this early hour and when she looked towards the white mountains of the Lefka Ori, they had a heat haze covering them. Eve spoke to her dog

'You've been a very good girl and haven't made a fuss at all with the changes in your routine. I'll take you for a nice long walk before I go to the hospital this morning.'

Portia wagged her tail as if she understood her mistress's every word.

'I don't know what I'd do without you, girl,' Eve said as a few tears filled her eyes.

She brushed them away, knowing that staying positive was the only thing that would get her through this. Her upbeat attitude had allowed her to survive the previous cases and she was determined to live to tell the tale of this one.

* * *

Just as Eve came back into the house after her walk with Portia, the phone started to ring. She quickly unhooked Portia's lead and rushed to answer it.

'Eve, it's Jane. I bumped into Kevin in the local shop and he told me everything; about David being kidnapped, about him escaping and getting pneumonia, and that now he's lost his memory. You must be sick with worry.'

'I am Jane, although I feel a little better today. I was overtired yesterday, but somehow I managed to get a good night's sleep. At least the police have put a guard outside David's ward in case the kidnappers come to the hospital.'

'I'm sure they'll keep him safe,' Jane remarked, trying to sound convincing.

However Eve wasn't at all certain that David would be safe now, not until the kidnappers were caught and dealt with.

'Well, Jane,' Eve said, wanting to change the subject so that she wouldn't start agonising too much again, 'you're off back to England very soon. Are you excited?'

'Yes and no. I'm going to miss this place.'

'But you will be back, won't you? Apart from coming to my wedding next summer.'

'Yes, hopefully at Christmas. Still, I feel a bit sad.' Jane paused for a moment.

'Eve, can I ask you something?'

'Of course. Ask me anything.'

'Paul left me with a couple of boxes before he went to jail. They're full of his paperwork and things from his real mother, Jennifer Anderson. He didn't want Kevin to see any of it. He said he didn't trust him any more, ever since Kevin found out that he had had an affair with Lucy. I don't know what he expects Kevin to do. I doubt if there's anything in the boxes that Kevin would find useful. He knows Paul asked me to look after some things for him so I don't want to take any chances. It's possible that he might break into my house while I'm away.'

'So, what do you want me to do, look

after the boxes for you?'

'Yes, please.'

'Fine. I'll put them in the basement. They should be safe down there.'

As Eve put the phone down and turned around, Robert and Alison appeared.

'Breakfast, you two?' Eve asked.

'Don't worry, Eve, we can get our own,' Alison replied with a smile.

When Alison had arrived the previous evening, she had thought how drained Eve looked. It wasn't at all surprising after everything that had gone on, but she was used to seeing Eve take control of every situation. It was obvious that David's kidnapping had taken a toll on her.

'Don't be silly,' Eve said. 'You're my guests so come and sit down.'

Robert and Alison thought it best to acquiesce. Eve was very much on edge so it seemed best to do as she wanted.

'So, how was Betty last night?' Eve asked.

'She was very strange. She kept

contradicting herself, one minute saying how much better off she was without Don and the next, bursting into tears because he had left her,' Alison admitted.

'Well, I think she put the last nail in the coffin when she went to the police back in June and told them that she thought her husband had had an affair with the murder victim.'

'She didn't, did she?' Alison exclaimed. 'But why would she do that?'

'I'm not sure. Their marriage was already shaky at the time and I think she was trying to implicate Don in the murder case. However, Don has told me that she really does think he was having an affair, and she still thinks he's having one now.'

'Who with?'

'She wouldn't say,' Eve replied.

'No wonder Don is fed up,' Alison stated. 'Perhaps it's a good thing they've split up. They are getting old and it would be awful if they spent the rest of their lives together feeling miserable. It is a surprise though that Don went to the hospital to help Betty.'

'Don is a good man and I'm sure he doesn't wish her ill,' Eve said.

'It beats me how he's stayed with her for so long,' Robert added. 'Sorry, Alison, but she is absolutely frightful.'

'She can be nice you know, Rob.'

'Well, I've yet to see it.'

'I presume you're going to be in the hospital most of today, Alison?' Eve asked.

'Yes, and I'm sure you will be too, Eve.'

'And where does that leave me?' Robert asked, half in jest. 'I don't know why I came over, I really don't.'

'Oh stop moaning, Robert,' Eve said. 'You came to help me, although things have worked out a little differently. You could take Portia for another walk later on. I've neglected her a bit the last few days.'

Robert nodded. It wouldn't be that bad if he had to hold the fort at home. He could work on his tan after all.

When he had come over the previous summer, Eve had asked him to help her search for the murderer. He hadn't got in nearly as much sunbathing as he wanted. Now here was his chance.

* * *

A couple of hours later, Alison was sitting with Betty and Eve was with David.

Betty was having her hip operation that morning and she was extremely nervous.

'Don said he'd be over this morning,' Betty remarked with a loud sigh. 'It doesn't surprise me that he hasn't turned up. That man cares nothing for me, nothing at all.'

Alison thought it best to let Betty rant as she wished. There was no point contradicting her. She always thought she was right.

Eve had been relieved to see that there was still a police officer outside David's ward and she was even more pleased when she saw David sitting up, looking a little better than he had the previous day.

'Darling, it's so good to see you looking brighter,' Eve gushed, kissing him. 'I've been so anxious. Have you got your memory back yet?'

'I remember a few things, but nothing of importance,' he admitted.

'Well, it's a start,' she said taking his hand. 'So what's come back to you?'

'I can recall being somewhere without windows, although the light was on at times. It must have been a basement. And I had my hands and feet tied up and a gag in my mouth, but I don't remember much else.'

'That's alright,' Eve said. 'If your memory has started to come back, hopefully you'll remember everything in time.'

'I know there's a policeman outside,' David continued. 'Is that really necessary? I mean, the police have enough to do.'

'Of course it's necessary,' Eve replied

sternly. 'The kidnappers might try to silence you.'

'Why?' David asked.

'Because you may have recognised one of them . . . or both.'

'I still feel like a fraud. Whoever they are, they may have left the island. It wouldn't surprise me.'

'The police suspect Pete Davies.'

'What?' David exclaimed. 'Never, we're good friends. He wouldn't do anything like that. I'll have to put them straight.'

'I don't think it's him either, but he did disappear the night before last and was found with a broken knee cap.'

'No, I still don't believe it. Poor Annie. What must she be going through?'

Eve nodded, but she was concerned. What if Pete did turn out to be the kidnapper? Annie's life would be as good as over and Eve certainly didn't want that for her.

* * *

After spending a couple of hours with David, Eve decided to go and see Pete. Entering his ward, she saw Annie first, sitting in a chair fast asleep. Pete noticed Eve and beckoned her over.

'How are you today, Pete?' Eve whispered, not wanting to wake Annie.

'I'm not doing so badly. I don't think I'll be here as long as I thought, though, but I wish I could say I'd be going home. I'm pretty certain the police are going to arrest me as soon as I leave here.'

Pete glanced at Annie.

'Poor Annie, she's so tired and scared. I wish she'd go home and rest. There's nothing she can do here.'

'She's obviously very upset, poor thing,' Eve replied. 'But I'm sure she has nothing to be nervous about. I mean, fancy the police thinking you kidnapped David. It's crazy. You and he go back a long way.'

'I don't think the police have a leg to stand on. They have no actual proof, but I just wish David would get his memory back so I can be cleared. I promise you, Eve, I had nothing to do with this.'

'I believe you, Pete, and David is adamant it wasn't you. He's starting to get his memory back by the way, but all he remembers so far is that he was in a basement somewhere. It's hopeful though. Perhaps by the end of the day, his memory will have returned.'

Annie woke up suddenly and seeing Eve tried to smile.

'Perhaps you should take Annie off for a cup of coffee, Eve,' Pete said.

'No, I can't leave you,' Annie said plaintively.

'Yes, you can,' Pete insisted.

'OK,' Annie replied. 'I feel I should go and see Betty as well.'

'I suppose I should too,' Eve said. 'Not that she'll appreciate it. Let's get a coffee first and then we'll go and see her.'

* * *

Less than an hour later the two women entered Betty's ward.

'How are you feeling?' Annie asked sympathetically. 'Are you having your op today?'

'I was, but they've cancelled it. It should be tomorrow now, but I'm having serious doubts. Honestly, this is getting quite ridiculous. They can't just leave me here in this pain. I'm not pleased, not pleased at all.'

Eve snapped at her attitude.

'You know, Betty, you should count your lucky stars that you're having this operation at all. So many Greeks have lost their jobs and their health care. They're literally dying because they can't afford to see a doctor or buy their medications.'

For once, Betty didn't retort in her usual forthright manner.

'You're right, Eve, I'm in so much pain that I can't think straight.'

Eve was shocked that Betty agreed with her, but doubted that this would be the start of a beautiful friendship.

'Haven't they given you painkillers?' Eve asked, softening her voice.

'Yes, but they wear off too quickly. How's David by the way?' she asked Eve.

'He's better today and is starting to get his memory back.'

'Has he remembered who kidnapped him?'

'Not yet, but it hopefully won't be long before everything comes back.'

After a few more pleasantries, the two women took their leave.

'Well, I'd never have credited it,' Alison remarked as soon as they had left.

'What?' Betty replied.

'You and Eve were actually talking civilly to each other.'

'Well, she must be extremely worried about David. Mind you, he wouldn't have got into all this trouble if it wasn't for her,' she added, tutting.

'Aunt Betty, that's a terrible thing to say.'

'Well, it's true. Whoever kidnapped

him is desperate for money and he was the ideal choice. Eve's got more money than sense. It's a pity they didn't kidnap her instead.'

Alison shook her head. The truce between Betty and Eve had lasted just a few minutes.

* * *

Eve bumped into Don on her way back to David's ward.

'I've just been to see Betty,' Eve remarked. 'She's a bit fed up that they aren't doing her operation today.'

'Yes, she didn't stop moaning when they told her. I was hoping she might have calmed down by now.'

'How are you, Don? Holding up?'

'I'm fine. I've moved back into the house for a little while.'

'Oh,' was all Eve could think of saying. Poor Don, he was being pulled back into that awful woman's grasp.

'Don't worry, I'm not getting back together with Betty,' Don said, as if reading Eve's mind. 'It just seemed to make sense while she wasn't there . . . and there's the cat as well of course, William.'

Eve smiled and although she didn't say anything, she was relieved. Don deserved some happiness and he certainly wasn't going to get it if he went back to Betty.

Having said their goodbyes, Eve continued on to see David. When she arrived, she saw Kevin was there and her heart sank, imagining that Joanna was probably around. However, she put on a smile and greeted Kevin as pleasantly as she could.

'Don't worry, Joanna's not here,' Kevin said quickly. 'We're not joined at the hip, you know, much as I wish we were.'

Both Kevin and David laughed, but Eve frowned. She was becoming more and more certain that Joanna was using Kevin for some other purpose. After all, as much as Eve didn't want to admit it, Joanna was beautiful and only in her early thirties. She could have someone richer, younger and better-looking than Kevin.

'I've remembered a few more things, Eve,' David announced.

'You have? That's great.'

However, she wished he wouldn't tell her what they were in front of Kevin, but there was nothing she could do about it.

'I remember coming out of the loo and tackling the kidnapper. That's when he fell and hit his head. Then I escaped.'

'Do you remember who it was?' Kevin asked.

Eve watched Kevin to see if he looked guilty, but his face was expressionless.

'No, that's still a blank.'

'I'm sure it will all come back when you're feeling better,' Kevin stated.

'I hope you're right,' Eve replied. 'You're not safe until then, David.'

She glanced at Kevin whose face still wasn't giving anything away.

* * *

The day proved to be very hectic for David. News of what had happened spread like wildfire throughout the villages and David had a stream of visitors. After Kevin left, Ken from The Black Cat arrived with food from the bar. David had very little appetite, but when he saw the succulent pork accompanied by roast potatoes, an enormous Yorkshire pudding and an array of vegetables, he had to try some. The food was so dire in the hospital that he had barely eaten anything since he had arrived. However, Jan Stewart's food was always so delicious that it did persuade him to make the effort to eat.

'I'm glad to see you eating a bit, darling,' Eve said, giving him a kiss on the cheek.

'I didn't think I was hungry, but this is still warm and very tasty. I reckon I can manage a little.'

While he was eating, Pete came hobbling in on crutches, with Annie who was fussing over him.

'I don't think you should be trying to walk so soon, Pete,' Annie said, concerned that her husband might fall over and end up with even more injuries.

'I have to speak to David,' he replied. 'I have to clear the air.'

David saw Pete hovering close to another bed and called him over.

'David I had to see you,' Pete said, sighing with relief as he sat down. It had been more difficult to walk than he had expected.

'I told him he should stay in bed,' Annie spoke. 'And what a palaver getting in here. We were searched and had to give all our contact details.'

'The police are very worried about David; that's why they're grilling everyone who comes in,' Eve said, sounding a little anxious. 'They think the kidnappers might try to get to David in here.'

Pete started talking directly to David. 'I swear to you that it wasn't me. I didn't kidnap you. Everything has just been a coincidence.'

'You don't have to explain yourself, Pete; I haven't thought for one minute that it was you. The police are grasping at straws because they can't find the real kidnappers and I can't remember much of what happened. They want to look as if they're getting somewhere with the case.'

'But if you don't remember who it was, the police will arrest Pete,' Annie said, tears filling her eyes.

'Hey, darling,' Pete said, trying to comfort her. 'You're not going to get rid of me that easily.'

'I'm remembering things slowly, and everything is a bit hazy, though I think the kidnapper who brought me food wore a mask. I just can't recognise him.'

'Or her,' Eve added.

'You're not still thinking it's Joanna, are you?' David asked.

'You should be satisfied after the other night,' Annie put in. 'I wish it was her so Pete would be in the clear, but you couldn't find David at either of the houses.'

David and Pete looked at each other, while Eve looked away.

Damn, now David's going to know about me breaking into Joanna's houses. He'll go mad.

'What happened the other night, Eve,' David asked sternly.

Eve hurriedly told him of her breaking into both of Joanna's properties and waited for him to tell her off.

'Oh, Eve,' David said. 'You are going to get into serious trouble one of these days if you carry on involving yourself in every crime. However,' he continued, taking Eve's hand, 'I think I would probably feel a bit hurt if you hadn't done something to help find me.'

Eve bent over and kissed David. He would probably want to give Eve a little talking to and Annie also wanted to tell Pete about her involvement, so it was time that they left. She knew Pete wouldn't be happy, but she hated keeping secrets from her husband.

After Annie and Pete had gone, it wasn't long before Jane visited and later Robert and Alison popped in as well. David felt quite tired by the time mid-afternoon came and was quite glad to have a rest while Eve read.

* * *

In the early evening, David watched Eve almost dropping off, still with a book in her hands.

'Darling, it's time for you to go home,' he said, giving her a gentle shake. 'You can barely keep your eyes open.'

'I have to stay with you. You're sick and you never know, you may remember something.'

'If I remember anything more, I'll phone Dimitris Kastrinakis straight away; I promise. You need rest and so do I. I love having you here, but I feel I have to stay awake.'

Eve frowned.

'And don't get upset by what I'm

saying. You know I'm right.'

'OK,' Eve said. 'But I'll be back first thing in the morning.'

David gently squeezed Eve's hand and she tried to smile. She was worried sick. Pneumonia killed a lot of people and just because he was feeling a bit better didn't mean he was out of the woods yet.

16

A little later that evening in the hospital, the nurses came round with medication for the patients and David was put on his regular dose of oxygen. He didn't much like having a mask on his face although he wasn't quite sure why. He normally wouldn't be bothered. Perhaps it was because he had been locked up and the mask made him feel claustrophobic.

As much as he wanted to carry on as normal, he had to concede to himself that this experience was going to change him.

A couple of hours later, a nurse came round to give David an injection. It wasn't one of his usual nurses, but she seemed pleasant enough. He didn't even bother asking what the injection was for. They had been giving him so many different treatments and he trusted the nursing staff. After all, they knew what was best for him.

Not long after the nurse had left David's bedside, he started to feel sick and dizzy. As it started getting worse, he tried to get out of bed to go to the bathroom, but as his feet touched the ground, he fell into a heap on the floor. There was blood coming out of his nose and then he was sick. He managed to get his head up to look around, but he had become delirious and didn't realise he was in hospital.

Luckily a couple of his ward companions saw him and started to ring their emergency bells frantically. A nurse arrived a moment later and found David on the floor. She felt his pulse and although he was still breathing, he looked as white as a sheet. She rushed out of the ward calling for help, at which time the police officer ran in. Seeing David on the floor he rang Dimitris Kastrinakis. Maybe this was part of his illness, but if not, someone had made an attempt to murder David Baker.

* * *

Eve sat by David's bedside. He was fast asleep, having had his stomach pumped. He had woken up when Eve came into the ward, but it hadn't taken him long to fall asleep again. His body had been through so much in the past few days and Eve wondered if he could take any more.

When the hospital had rung her earlier, Eve had panicked, but she had managed to calm down enough to cope with the half an hour drive to get there. She had very sensibly not had any alcohol once she had got home from the hospital, just in case she had to go back again. In her rush to get out of the house, she forgot to let Robert and Alison know about this turn of events.

Eve couldn't stop looking at David. He was so pale, even his tan seemed to have faded. She couldn't help but blame herself.

If David hadn't met me, none of this would have happened. I'm no good for him. Perhaps I should pack my bags and go back home to England. Then he might find himself a nice quiet girl who wouldn't cause him any more problems.

Eve really meant this as she thought it, but a few minutes later her tune had changed.

'David, darling, please wake up. I can't live without you. My life would be meaningless.'

Eve heard someone cough behind her and she turned to see Dimitris Kastrinakis standing there.

'He's not too good, Inspector,' Eve said straight away. 'You won't be able to talk to him at the moment.'

'It's you I'd like to speak to, Miss Masters. Perhaps we can talk in the corridor.'

'Oh, alright,' she replied. 'Not that I can tell you much. When I left the hospital earlier on, David was much better. He was still having his oxygen at regular intervals of course, but he was sitting up.'

'The doctors should know soon what sort of poison he was given.'

'Poison!' Eve exclaimed. 'David's been poisoned? Someone wanted him dead?'

Eve felt a few tears in her eyes, but blinked a couple of times to get rid of them. One thing she refused to do was cry in front of Dimitris.

'Yes, the symptoms he had were synonymous with poisoning,' Dimitris continued, feeling a little sorry for Eve. Yes, she was an interfering busybody, but she hadn't caused any of this.

'It's all my fault. If David hadn't got involved with me, he wouldn't have been kidnapped.'

'Now, now, Miss Masters; it doesn't do any good blaming yourself. It's not your fault. Somebody desperate for money thought they could get it from you.'

'Yes I know,' Eve replied, 'but they chose David because he's my fiancé and I have the money to pay them off . . . But why on earth would they do this?'

'My guess is that they're worried that he might remember who one of them is. Even if he wore a mask, David might have still recognised the voice and shape of the person.'

'But what do we do now?' Eve asked in exasperation. 'Whoever it is managed to get into the ward, even with an officer standing guard.'

'We will have to carry on the way we are. There's not much else we can do. Hopefully when David wakes up, he will remember who kidnapped him and we can arrest that person.'

The doctor came up to Eve and Dimitris.

'Have you any news, doctor,' Eve asked. 'Do you know what poisoned David?'

Dimitris indicated that it was alright for Eve to hear the news.

'Well, we found arsenic trioxide in his system.'

'Arsenic trioxide!' Eve exclaimed. 'That was what James Anderson gave Paul, Jane and me earlier in the year. I didn't think it could kill you; just make you very ill.'

'A large dose can kill and perhaps he would have died if we hadn't pumped his stomach so quickly after it had been administered,' the doctor replied. 'It's a good job there were other patients in the ward who called for help.'

'Oh my goodness,' Eve cried out. 'This just gets worse. How on earth could anyone get in to give it to him?'

'I don't know, Miss Masters,' Dimitris said. 'The officer checked everyone going into the ward . . . What would have been the best way to administer the drug, doctor?'

'It's normally injected into the vein, but over one to two hours. I would imagine that whoever gave this to him, injected a larger dosage quickly. Alternatively, it could be ingested with food.

The food would smell garlicky so you may not be aware you are taking it into your system. I'm sure none of our nurses tried to kill Mr Baker, so I have no idea how he or she got past the security you have set up.'

What security? Eve said to herself. *One policeman wouldn't stop the killers if they were determined to get rid of my David.*

'Will he be alright, doctor?' was all Eve said in the end.

'He's a strong and fit man and in normal circumstances he would probably improve very soon, but the pneumonia unfortunately makes it all a bit more difficult for him to recover at the speed we would expect.'

The doctor soon left and Dimitris noticed how drained Eve looked.

'He doesn't sound that hopeful, does he?' Eve remarked.

'Now, now, Miss Masters, be positive. Mr Baker will need you to be strong for him.'

'Well, I'm staying the night here. It's

already half three in the morning anyway.'

'As you wish. If he wakes up and gives any indication of who kidnapped him, ring me, whatever time it is. Oh, one thing, what has Mr Baker eaten and drunk today?'

'He had very little appetite and didn't eat any of the hospital meals. I brought him a sandwich and he ate a few bites of that. Oh, I almost forgot, Ken the owner of The Black Cat brought him a meal and he ate quite a bit of it. It was pork, roast potatoes and some vegetables. I didn't notice a smell of garlic, but I don't suppose I would have thought anything of it.'

'Are the remains of this food here?'

'No, we threw them away as it was cold . . . You don't think Ken poisoned him?'

'It's a possibility, but if the food has gone, there's no way to find out. How well do you know this Ken?'

'We do go into the bar quite a bit so I've talked to him lots of times. He and his wife, Jan, are very nice, but I think I told you that they're short of money.'

'Yes, I believe you did.'

A nurse was just about to go into the ward when she was stopped by the police officer on guard. Dimitris asked her of the possibility of the rubbish still being on the premises, but unfortunately it was collected late in the evening as was quite common on the island.

'Well, we shall question Ken and Jan Stewart tomorrow first thing. Remember Miss Masters, phone if you find out anything from Mr Baker.'

Eve nodded as Dimitris left and was just about to go back in the ward, when the truth suddenly hit her, or at least what she thought was the truth.

Joanna Neonakis is definitely involved. I know that now. What's more, she's the woman who collaborated with James Anderson and killed him. Arsenic trioxide was what James used on Jane, Paul and me. She used it to try and kill David. It's so obvious; I was right all along about Joanna.

* * *

Eve had been sitting beside David's bed for a few hours. She had hardly slept, hoping he'd wake up. She was also busy trying to work out how Joanna had got the arsenic trioxide into David's system. Perhaps she was involved with Ken and poor Jan knew nothing about it. That was one explanation.

No, she thought at about six the next morning. *Joanna must have come here, dressed up as a nurse or doctor and given it to David. There aren't that many people here later in the evening and that woman's as bold as brass. She could fool any police officer if she wanted.*

She wondered what she should do with this information. Dimitris Kastrinakis would probably think it was only conjecture and he'd be right. There was no point telling him anything. He already knew she thought Joanna was involved.

No, she'd just have to wait until David woke up and perhaps he'd be able to tell them what had really happened.

About half an hour later, David stirred and his eyes opened.

'David, my darling. Thank goodness. I was so scared I was going to lose you.'

He didn't have the energy to say much at first, but he took Eve's hand. She burst into tears and tried desperately to stop them. David needed her to be positive, not a mess.

'What happened?' he finally whispered, unable to talk any louder.

Eve didn't know whether to tell him that he had been poisoned. It might upset him and put back his recovery.

'Come on, Eve,' he continued, his voice recovering a little. 'Tell me the truth.'

He could see she was wavering, but he needed to know everything.

'OK David. Somebody tried to poison you.'

'What?'

'Yes, I think your kidnappers are afraid you'll remember who they are. Can you?'

'No, I'm sorry darling. I can't remember anything else. As for last night, everything is a blur. I can vaguely remember trying to get out of bed, falling on the floor and feeling sick, but that's it.'

Eve decided to take a risk and tell him her theory about Joanna and the arsenic trioxide.

'Oh Eve,' he said. 'Don't do anything silly.'

He was afraid that she would act recklessly again trying to prove that Joanna was involved.

'Don't you think it's a possibility then?' she asked finally.

'Yes, but it's all conjecture, so I think you're best off not telling the police.'

Eve nodded. She couldn't think what she could do anyway. It might be best if she didn't leave David's side until they caught the kidnappers, but would the police be clever enough to catch Joanna? Eve didn't think so.

17

At about nine o'clock that morning, Dimitris Kastrinakis came back to the hospital. He was pleased to see that David was awake, although he was disappointed that he hadn't remembered anything else.

'Mr Baker,' he asked. 'Can you tell us who came to your bedside after Miss Masters went home last night?'

'Not many people,' David replied. 'The nurses came with my medication and to give me more oxygen. Oh, then another nurse came in a couple of hours later to gave me an injection. It was the first injection I'd had and I have no idea what it was for.'

That's it, Eve thought, trying her best not to let her excitement show through. *Somebody dressed up as a nurse and came in and gave David the arsenic trioxide with a syringe — and that someone was Joanna; I'm sure of it.*

She said nothing however, knowing that Dimitris would tell her she was speculating too much.

Dimitris decided to go and check up on what medications David was supposed to be having, leaving David and Eve alone for a few minutes.

'David,' Eve said breathlessly. 'If Dimitris comes back and says you weren't supposed to have an injection, we'll know that somebody dressed up as a nurse in order to gain access to you. It must have been Joanna.'

'Eve, you could be right, but don't go trying to prove it. It's too dangerous, plus it might not be her after all, but somebody else.'

Eve nodded, but she was certain that David was wrong. She was convinced it was Joanna and she had to do something before that woman tried yet again to kill the man she loved.

* * *

It took about half an hour for Dimitris to return to David's ward. By this time Eve was getting impatient, feeling that she could be doing something more pro-active than just sitting with David doing nothing. Although she had said that she wouldn't leave him, she was now thinking that it might be the only way to catch the kidnappers. After all, the police were guarding David and more care would be taken today after the attempt on his life.

'Well,' Dimitris said as he came back into the ward. 'I've had it confirmed that you weren't supposed to have any injections. None of the nurses can remember seeing anyone different last night, but Kostas, the officer who was on duty in the evening, said a nurse came around at nine. She obviously convinced him that she had a viable reason for going in to see Mr Baker.'

'I knew it,' Eve exclaimed excitedly, jumping up. 'Is the police officer certain it was a woman?'

'Yes, Miss Masters.' Dimitris paused

for a moment as he realised that Eve was still certain who the person was. 'You're not thinking it was Joanna Neonakis, are you?'

Dimitris knew the answer before Eve spoke.

'Well, yes. I'm sorry you don't believe me, but I am certain,' Eve said, pouting. 'The more I think about it, the less I believe that the kidnapping was arranged by any of our close friends.'

David sighed. Eve was getting herself into hot water again.

'Please don't do anything irresponsible, Miss Masters,' Dimitris said. 'We will be questioning her, along with a number of other suspects, as to their movements last night, but even if Mrs Neonakis hasn't got an alibi, we can't arrest her just because you think it was her. By the way, Mr Baker, can you remember anything about the woman who gave you this injection?'

'I'm sorry; I didn't take much notice and I doubt if I would be able to recognise her.'

'She'd have put on a disguise anyway,' Eve chipped in. 'David knows Joanna and would recognise her otherwise.'

Dimitris shook his head slowly. Eve was becoming too involved again. He'd have to keep a close eye on her.

* * *

With Dimitris gone, Eve started to drift off to sleep. She was exhausted and desperately needed to catch up on some shut eye.

An hour later, Eve woke up with a start to see Robert chatting to David. She had rung him earlier to tell him what had happened during the night.

'Oh my goodness,' she exclaimed. 'I shouldn't have dropped off. Anybody could have crept in and tried to kill David.'

'Relax, Eve,' David said. 'The police are taking extra precautions now. It's time you went home and caught up with some sleep.'

'No, I can't leave you,' Eve exclaimed.

'I'll stay with David, Eve,' Robert said gently. 'I think Alison's going to be with Betty for a while today anyway.'

'OK,' Eve said reluctantly. 'But I'll be back later though.'

David smiled. 'I'll see you when you've had a good long sleep then, darling. But only if you're up to it. It might be better if you rested until tomorrow. Now remember, don't do anything about Joanna. If it was her who tried to kill me, she's a very dangerous woman.'

* * *

While he was in the hospital, Dimitris decided to go and question Annie Davies. Her husband, Pete, was still a suspect despite both Eve and David not believing that he could be the kidnapper. Now Dimitris wondered if his wife could be his co-conspirator. Of course, she would have to be a good actress considering the way she had behaved the past few days. However, nothing surprised Dimitris any more.

Both Pete and Annie were shocked to hear that David had been poisoned, but when Dimitris asked Annie where she had been the previous evening at around nine o'clock, Pete finally lost his temper.

'I'm getting fed up of this,' he raged. 'Now you're insinuating that Annie is one of the kidnappers. David is a very good friend of ours and we would never do him any harm, never.'

'I shall be questioning a lot of people, not just you,' Dimitris said. 'I have to ask these questions so that I can eliminate you from my enquiries.'

'Well, I'm afraid you won't be able to eliminate me,' Annie said wearily. 'I don't have an alibi. I stayed here until about eight and then I drove home on my own. I didn't see anyone so nobody can vouch for me.'

Annie watched the other officer, Stavros, write everything down. The walls were closing in on her and she felt she was going to be arrested on circumstantial evidence. She was tired and fed up of it all.

'Well, thank you, Mrs Davies,' Dimitris said. 'That'll be all for now.'

'And where do you think she got the drug from?' Pete asked the officer angrily.

He didn't want to leave things as they were.

'I've no idea,' Dimitris said. 'I'm not arresting your wife. I just came to ask these questions.'

'It's alright, Pete, he's just doing his job,' Annie put in.

There was no point antagonising the police. It would make them look guiltier.

'We will need to search your house though,' Dimitris added.

'You'll need a warrant for that,' Pete spoke, the policeman in him coming out.

'I know, but it's not difficult to get one. Now if you'll excuse me, I do have other people to question. As you see,

I've not singled you out,' he added before leaving the ward.

Pete was going to say more, but Annie put her hand on his arm to stop him. She knew the police wouldn't find anything at the house so it wasn't worth saying anything else or making a fuss.

* * *

Dimitris Kastrinakis and Stavros continued to have a busy morning. They obtained search warrants and looked over Pete and Annie's house, finding nothing to incriminate them.

The next stop was The Black Cat where Dimitris nearly came to blows with Ken Stewart.

'This is beyond belief,' Ken spoke angrily. 'First you suggest that I had poisoned David's food and then you imply that my wife dressed up as a nurse in order to give David a deadly dose of poison.'

'Shush, Ken,' Jan said. 'He's only doing his job. We're innocent so have nothing to worry about. I have an alibi anyway. Quite a few people saw me in the bar last night so I couldn't have been in the hospital.'

Nevertheless Dimitris and Stavros searched the premises before they left. Again they found nothing to suggest they were involved.

Their last stop was to see Joanna Neonakis. Dimitris wasn't looking forward to it after the reception he'd got from his other suspects, if that's what they really were. The English community was tight and it did seem unlikely that any of them would kidnap David Baker. At least that was one advantage of going to see Mrs Neonakis. She was an outsider and hadn't mingled with the English crowd much.

Arriving at her house, he rang the door bell and before long Joanna answered the door. She smiled sweetly at Dimitris and his colleague.

'Good afternoon, officers, how can I help you?' she asked politely.

'I am questioning a number of

people,' Dimitris said, not wanting her to feel singled out. 'It seems as if someone dressed up as a nurse last night and tried to kill Mr Baker.'

'Oh my goodness, how awful. Who-ever would have done that? You'd better come in. I take it you will want to search both my houses.'

Dimitris was stunned at her demeanour.

Perhaps Eve Masters is right after all. Joanna is much too calm and collected. It's as if she had this planned.

Dimitris and Stavros went into the house.

'Can I offer you and your officers anything to drink, Chief Inspector?' Joanna asked.

They both refused her offer and Dimitris went on to ask her where she had been at nine the previous evening.

'I'm afraid I haven't got an alibi. I was here alone,' she replied.

Dimitris marvelled at how composed she was.

'You don't seem worried that you

don't have an alibi.'

'Well, why should I worry? I'm innocent and I have no doubt that you will catch the right person. I doubt very much if you'll throw me into jail just because I don't have an alibi.'

Dimitris and Stavros did their search immediately after questioning her and then she took them to the other house. As he expected, he didn't find any arsenic trioxide or a nurse's outfit.

If she is the one who tried to kill David Baker, Dimitris thought, *she would have got rid of any evidence. She's clever, very clever. And so is Miss Masters. As much as I have resented her interfering in the murder cases, she seems to have an eye for criminals. Perhaps I should do a background check on Mrs Neonakis.*

18

Eve settled down on the sofa with Portia by her side, thinking how awful it would be not to have her dog with her.

She remembered when Phyllis Baldwin, the woman who murdered Jane's father, had poisoned Portia. It was lucky that she had got to the vet in time, otherwise the outcome might have been very different.

Eve shuddered, thinking how close to death David had also come not that many hours ago. She felt a couple of tears falling, but brushed them away, determined to remain strong.

Eve had picked up Paul's boxes from Jane on her way back from the hospital, but hadn't bothered to put them in the basement yet.

She decided she'd ask Robert to carry them down when he and Alison returned. They were going out for a meal after they left the hospital and had tried to persuade Eve to go with them. They'd even said they would pick her up, but she excused herself. She felt too tired and on edge to eat out.

Eve wasn't able to stop her mind running riot. She looked at the boxes, her curiosity aroused. She almost got up to have a look in one of them, but stopped herself. There'd be nothing of interest to her, would there? And anyway, she shouldn't look in other people's property. They belonged to Paul and he was in jail, still waiting for his trial date to come up. Bail had been set at some ridiculous amount and nobody had paid it. Eve thought it was a good job as he might have pestered poor Jane and that was the last thing the girl needed.

She went and poured herself a large glass of ice cold Chardonnay, deciding that if she had to go to the hospital again that day, she'd get a cab. She didn't think she was in the right frame of mind to drive, even without alcohol.

However, as Eve drank her wine, she kept looking at the boxes. In the end she had to take a peek, but just in one . . .

There were the usual papers for Paul's house and for Jennifer Anderson's, which he had inherited, a birth certificate, receipts and so on. Nothing was of particular interest to Eve. Then she found some photos.

This looks a bit more exciting, she thought, examining them more closely.

There were none of Crete. She remembered Paul getting a digital camera after Christmas and loading all the photos onto his computer. These were older and there were ones of a younger Paul, ones of Kevin and Lucy and their boys. Then Eve stopped. There were quite a few photos of Jennifer Anderson, obviously taken before Paul had met her. He must have taken them from her house when he was clearing it out. There were a couple with her nephew, James, but it was the other person in the photos that made her gasp out loud.

I don't believe it. It's her . . . Joanna. What on earth is she doing with James and Jennifer?

* * *

Half an hour later, Eve was still sitting on the floor, trying to decide what to do with the photos. She had thought of phoning Jane, but changed her mind. Jane would probably be angry that she had gone through Paul's things.

I bet you Jane won't have been nosey and had a look. She's always doing things by the book . . . So what are my options? she wondered.

She could take the photo to the police, though Dimitris might disregard it. After all, what did it prove? It proves Joanna knew Jennifer and James before she came to the island.

I must be right. She did kill James, but why? Perhaps I should ring Dimitris.

Eve went and got her mobile and dialled.

'Nai,' the voice on the other end said.

'Mr Kastrinakis, this is Eve Masters. I've found evidence that Joanna and James Anderson knew each other.'

'What sort of evidence, Miss Masters?' he asked, wondering what illegal act she had performed to get this information.

'I have a photo of them together with Jennifer Anderson,' she replied.

'Really,' he commented, deciding not to ask where she had got the photo from. It didn't matter much. 'And what do you want me to do with this? It doesn't prove that she killed James Anderson or that she's the kidnapper.'

'No,' Eve replied, 'but it's a bit suspicious if you ask me.'

'I'm sorry Miss Masters, there's no law stating that you have to tell everyone your business. I suggest you forget about it and get some rest. Leave the detecting to us. I did notice how tired you were looking today.'

Eve went quiet on the other end which prompted Dimitris to continue speaking.

'Now, one bit of advice for you, Miss Masters. Please keep away from Mrs Neonakis. You're lucky she hasn't filed a complaint against you.'

'Fine,' Eve said sharply. 'Thanks for nothing.' With that, Eve ended the call.

She was furious with him. Shouldn't he have agreed to go and question Joanna about her relationship with James? It was all connected, but she had yet to discover how. Couldn't Dimitris see that?

Eve then wondered if she should go and visit Paul in jail and ask what the relationship was. However, he wouldn't be happy if he knew that Eve had been poking her nose into his belongings.

No, the only thing I can do is confront Joanna herself. However, she is a dangerous woman and could do something to make me keep quiet about the whole thing. I could of course leave a note for Robert. If I'm not back when he returns, I'll tell him to come and find me.

Eve got changed and then looked in the mirror. She was shocked when she saw her reflection. She couldn't look like this in front of Joanna.

As Eve did her make-up, she started to tremble.

Perhaps I shouldn't do this. David would go mad if he knew what I was about to do, but if I don't his life will remain in danger. He'll be looking over his shoulder all the time. The kidnappers won't give up as there's every chance he'll get his memory back.

Eve went and got a pad of paper and a pen. She wrote quickly.

Have evidence that Joanna knew James. I've gone to confront her. If not home when you read this, come and find me or ring the police.

She went and put it on the fridge door. Robert was continually going to the fridge and she had no doubt he'd want a drink before bed. She then wondered if she should take Portia with her for protection, but then decided against it. Joanna could easily kill the dog and she didn't want to risk Portia's life again.

Eve filled up Portia's food and water bowls, took her bag and left the house, hoping against hope that she would return safely later that evening.

* * *

As she had been drinking wine, Eve decided to be sensible and walk to Joanna's house. It was only a twenty minute stroll and Eve planned to use the time to decide what she was going to say.

However, by the time she reached Joanna's home, she hadn't made up her mind what approach to take. And what if Kevin was there? He was probably her co-conspirator, even though she was having trouble believing it. David and Kevin had become good friends, so perhaps she had a different associate in crime. It wouldn't surprise her at all. Or perhaps she had done it all on her own, but how could she have kidnapped David? She was such a slim woman — but perhaps she had a gun to threaten him with.

Reaching the front door, Eve knocked. Within seconds Joanna came to the door.

'Oh, it's you,' Joanna said. 'What do you want?' she demanded.

She wasn't nearly as courteous to Eve as she had been to the police officers.

'I just wanted a word with you. Can I come in?'

'Fine. You know where the sitting room is from your last visit,' she said sarcastically, 'so do go and make yourself at home. I'm going to get a glass of wine from the kitchen. Do you want one?'

Eve hesitated.

'Hah,' Joanna laughed. 'You think I'm going to poison you. Well come into the kitchen and watch me pour the wine into the glasses. They'll be from the same bottle.'

Eve almost declined as it looked too obvious that she didn't trust Joanna, but she didn't want to take the risk. She also desperately needed a drink to get through this visit, so she followed Joanna into the kitchen and watched while she poured out their drinks.

Sitting down in the lounge, Eve made sure Joanna drunk first before taking a sip herself. It was a very nice wine, a Chablis; so much better than the local stuff.

'So, what do you want to talk to me about?' Joanna asked. 'The police have already been here today.'

'I don't want to ask you anything about David. I just want to know about your relationship with James Anderson.'

Joanna looked stunned for a moment and it didn't escape Eve. However, she regained her composure very quickly, but Eve could tell that this wasn't the question Joanna had been expecting.

'How did you find out that I know James? Not that it proves anything.'

Eve decided to be liberal with the truth.

'Paul Fowler left some boxes with Jane, his ex-girlfriend, to look after. She asked me to keep them safe as she's going back to England. I was putting them away and a few photos fell out of one box. There were a couple of you, James and Jennifer Anderson.'

'Really?' Joanna remarked. 'I reckon you looked through them and found these photos.'

'That is not something I would do,' Eve protested, putting her acting skills to good use.

'Well, it doesn't matter either way really, although I reckon that you are a nosey and interfering busybody.'

'I'm just making sure that David doesn't get hurt again. You are my number one suspect . . . oh, and by the way, I rang the police before I came, so they'll know it's you if I'm found injured or dead,' she added.

All of a sudden, Joanna pulled out a gun and Eve jumped.

'I think we should leave now. Get up,' Joanna demanded, pointing the gun at Eve.

Eve took a long gulp of wine and stood up. Just as she did, the door opened and Kevin came in. Joanna turned and pointed her gun at him.

'Whoa, what's going on here?'

Eve thought Kevin sounded as if he didn't know what Joanna was doing with a gun. Perhaps he had nothing to do with the kidnapping after all.

'How did you get in?' Joanna asked.

'You gave me a key so I could clear out all the furniture once you'd gone back to England.'

'I didn't mean you to use it now. We're hardly having an affair.'

'I thought things were going well between us.'

'They were, but you just had to go and spoil things, didn't you?' she hissed.

Eve listened to their conversation, finally realising that Kevin didn't know anything at all about David's kidnapping.

‘Well Kevin, we’re leaving. You’re going to drive your car with Eve in the seat next to you. I will sit in the back. If you don’t do what I tell you, I will shoot you. Do you understand? You must follow my instructions to the letter.’

Both Eve and Kevin nodded. As they walked towards the car, she realised that her plan hadn’t worked. Even if Robert or the police turned up at Joanna’s house, they wouldn’t find her there.

* * *

A few moments later, they were in the car and Kevin turned the engine on.

‘Now drive, Kevin. I’ll tell you where to turn.’

‘We’re not going to the other house then?’ he asked, looking in his mirror at the woman in the back seat.

‘Do you think I’m stupid? If by any chance Eve really did ring the police to say where she was going, they’re bound to look in the other house as well. Or perhaps you left a message for someone else, too?'

'No,' Eve replied. 'I thought we could talk sensibly, Joanna.'

'Then you're a fool, Eve Masters, but I think you may be lying. Now, get a move on, Kevin.'

Kevin was trembling, wondering how he had allowed himself to be drawn into Joanna's web. She had just been using him, though what for he didn't know. How could he have been fooled by her? How could he think that she really liked him? She was beautiful and not much older than thirty. He didn't think he was that bad looking, but he was old enough to be her father.

Kevin stalled the car twice, neither time on purpose, not that Joanna believed him.

'Do you want me to shoot you here, Kevin? Just get driving or I damn well will kill you.'

Luckily he managed to get the car going the third time and he started driving, Joanna giving him instructions to turn left or right every now and then. Eve stayed quiet throughout the whole journey, realising that she had underestimated Joanna. The woman was clever, there was no doubt about it and Eve had got herself into another mess. This time David couldn't help her. Was this going to be the end?

'You're very quiet, Eve Masters,' Joanna spoke a little later.

'Not a lot to say, is there?' Eve responded.

'To think I got one over the great private detective,' Joanna laughed.

Eve refused to comment. She was probably right and this could be the end. She would be murdered in cold blood and this time she couldn't think of a way out of the mess.

* * *

After about twenty minutes, they arrived at a house. Eve and Kevin weren't quite sure where they were.

Joanna had taken them on a strange journey, sometimes going down roads twice and then driving on roads which neither of them knew. Eve realised Joanna was trying to confuse them.

The house was in complete darkness and both Kevin and Eve had no idea who it belonged to or exactly where they were.

'Which village is this?' Eve asked, not really expecting to be told.

'Oh, I don't think you need to know that, Eve. This is just the empty house where David was kept before he escaped. I was stupid leaving my partner to deal with the day to day running of the plan, but that's over and done with now, so let's get back to the present. Kevin, give me the car keys and slowly get out at the same time as me. I don't want to have to shoot you. Whatever you may think, I did enjoy my time with you. Oh, and by the way, both of you give me your mobile phones,' she demanded, holding out her hand. 'I can't have you ringing for help when I'm gone.'

Once they did this, Kevin got out of the car with Joanna. She had the gun pointed at him the whole time. Eve vaguely thought of doing a runner, but discarded that idea quickly. She had no doubt at all that Joanna would attempt to shoot her.

After Eve had also got out of the car, Joanna told them both to walk towards the house.

Once there, she instructed Kevin to open the door with the key she had given him.

Eve felt sick. Was Joanna going to murder them inside the house and leave their bodies to rot?

Once the door was open, Joanna instructed Eve and Kevin to walk down into the basement. Eve had an awful feeling that she was right. Joanna was going to kill them.

'You still haven't told me what your relationship to James was?' Eve asked the other woman, hoping to stall her.

'You're wasting time, I know that, but

I'll tell you anyway.'

Kevin looked flabbergasted.

'I didn't know that you knew James.'

'I haven't told you everything.'

'Yes . . . I don't feel as if I know you at all, Joanna,' Kevin muttered.

'Of course you don't. I've only told you what you needed to know . . . and some of it, I made up.' She laughed while Kevin looked horrified.

'So, tell us about you and James,' Eve insisted once again.

'He was my husband. We were supposed to be Jennifer's sole heirs, half of her estate going to each of us, but then Paul turned up. That got us worried. After all, there was now a distinct possibility that she might change her will. She had two houses and a bit of cash and it would have seen us alright for a couple of years. Then before Christmas, she told James that she was going to leave a third of her estate to Paul and she'd be making the new will in the New Year. We were naturally upset and that's when I came up with the plan to kill her. Well, you know the rest. It didn't work out quite the way we intended.'

'And you killed your own husband?' Eve asked, although she already knew the answer.

'James gambled a lot. He was more of a hindrance than a help in our marriage.'

'You could have divorced him instead of killing him,' Eve replied.

'I could have done, but he'd botched things up, not to mention the fact that he was wasting the little money we had on gambling. By the time a divorce would have come through, there'd have been no money left at all. Plus I imagine that he would have been pestering me forever if he had lived; in fact, I'm sure of it.'

'So you were the woman in the hotel room in Athens?' Eve asked.

'I was, but I used a different name and a fake passport. I disappeared straight after killing James and then went home and pretended I hadn't been anywhere. I intended to claim my husband's share of Jennifer's will, but the evil bitch had already changed it and left everything to Paul.'

'Well, he was her son,' Eve stated.

'Trust you to take his side. Now he has another two houses and quite a bit of cash. But he's in prison so what good is it to him? I could definitely have used that money.'

'I would imagine it will come in handy for Paul — he has to have a defence lawyer and they don't come cheap.'

'What's the point? He's already admitted that he killed Lucy and Yiannis so they might as well skip over the trial.'

Eve was starting to get annoyed. Even though Paul had killed two people, they had become friends and she didn't want to see him treated badly by the Greek justice system. Goodness knows it was difficult enough being tried for murder; he needed a good lawyer to make sure the trial was above board.

'So, Joanna,' Eve said, deciding to change the subject. 'You haven't finished your story. How did you meet Yiannis?'

'Yiannis! Well, we'd actually met a few years ago when I came here for a holiday and we stayed in touch.'

'So you'd had an affair with him?' Kevin asked, finally able to speak. He had been shocked at seeing this side of Joanna and he was beginning to feel quite depressed. Kevin had thought that Joanna liked him, but it had all been a pretence.

'Well, I'd hardly call it an affair. Yiannis and I were adult enough not to ask anything from each other. In fact, he was a man after my own heart. He would have lots of relationships; well they were really just short-lived romances with girls on holiday. I certainly had no desire to settle down with him or with anyone else. I enjoyed my own little flings. However, when my scheme with James came to a sorry end, I had to think of other ways to keep myself afloat financially.'

'Didn't you consider getting a job?' Eve asked. 'That's what most people do. And anyway, I heard that you ran your own business.'

'I have a business, a boutique, but it hardly keeps me in the style I deserve. Yiannis had been to England a couple of times and we'd met, but when he told me he was coming earlier in the year, I formed a plan, a plan to make him want me more than any other woman. I pulled out all the stops and it worked. He fell for me in a way you can't imagine. Yiannis, the womaniser, was under my spell and when he asked me to marry him, I jumped at the chance. I had no idea that my plan would work as well as it did, but I wasn't going to wait. We got married and I intended to sell my business to come out and live with him.'

'So you fell for him too?' Eve asked.

'Not really,' Joanna said. 'I'd always enjoyed his company and we were good in bed together . . . '

Kevin cringed. He had been trying to get Joanna to sleep with him since they'd met, but with no success. However, she had been to bed with Yiannis many times even though she knew he bedded many other women. She obviously wasn't fussy, so why did she keep rejecting him?

'Am I so unattractive to you, Joanna?' Kevin asked suddenly.

It was now Eve's turn to cringe. Poor Kevin, he must have a wish to be humiliated lurking somewhere in that brain of his.

His own wife had a thing going with Yiannis as well, Eve thought. *What on earth had women seen in him? He had been completely obnoxious*.

'Oh, I do like you Kevin,' Joanna gushed, 'and I probably would have slept with you eventually and possibly even have married you if a better idea hadn't entered my mind.'

'What are you, some sort of black widow?' Eve asked, unable to hide her distaste. 'Did you just want these men for their money?'

'Well, seeing as you won't be getting out of here anytime soon, I can be honest. I did intend to eventually get rid of Yiannis. After all, it would have made me a fairly rich widow; no, what am I saying? It *has* made me quite a rich widow. Everybody thought I was only trying to sell the smaller house, the one belonging to Yiannis' parents, but I've sold the other one in a private sale. It went through a few days ago and the money is already sitting in my bank account outside the country.'

'It won't do you much good when you're rotting in jail,' Eve said, glaring at Joanna.

'Who says I'm going to jail? They won't find you here that quickly, you know.'

'What do you mean?' Kevin asked. 'You're not going to leave us here to die . . . are you?'

Kevin's voice was trembling and Eve wondered if he was going to cry.

Oh, for goodness sake, Kevin, get a

grip, Eve thought angrily.

If David had been there, he would have grabbed the gun ages ago and wrestled that awful woman to the floor.

'Now, Eve, get those bits of rope and tie up Kevin's hands and feet. I will check they're tight enough before I go.'

'And what if I refuse?' Eve asked.

'I'll kill you now. I don't really want to kill anybody else, but if I have to, I will.'

'You're going to kill us anyway by leaving us in here to die slowly.'

'I didn't say I was going to leave you in this house to die, did I? I will get in touch with someone eventually to let you out. I'll be long gone by then.'

'It was you, wasn't it? You dressed up as a nurse and injected my David with arsenic trioxide. It didn't work though, did it? He's still alive.'

'I was sure I gave him enough to kill him, but I made a mistake. Like I made a mistake in my choice of accomplice.'

Who on earth is she working with? Eve mused, desperate to find out.

Instead she said something completely different.

'What about the other house, Joanna. You'll lose money there. You can't exactly leave a forwarding address for the funds to be sent to.'

'That's life. I think my adventures on Crete are over. It's time to move on.'

'You haven't done nearly as well as you hoped, have you, Joanna? I mean you got nothing from me in the end, did you?'

'Eve,' Kevin whispered. 'Shut up.'

'Yes, keep quiet, Eve Masters, the great detective, otherwise I might just kill you now.'

Eve knew she was trying her luck and decided to do exactly as Joanna asked. She tied up Kevin's feet and hands and then Joanna told her to tie up her own feet.

'Now put your hands behind your back and I'll tie them.'

Having checked that the ropes were secure, Joanna spoke to them for one last time.

'Well, I won't delay any longer. Don't worry; you won't be here for too long.'

With that, Joanna left them and they heard the key turn and a bolt being pushed across the door.

'What do we do now?' Kevin asked Eve, looking shocked.

'If you were anything like my David, you would have managed to get the gun off Joanna and she would be the one tied up, not us.'

'I didn't see you trying anything,' he replied, sounding disconcerted.

'I wouldn't have trusted you to back me up.'

'Eve,' Kevin said. 'Let's stop this bickering. It looks like we're going to be here for some time.'

'Yes, you're right. I still wonder why she didn't kill us though.'

'Maybe she's not all bad.'

'Kevin, she killed her own husband because she was annoyed with him.'

Kevin just grunted, but inside he knew that he'd had a lucky escape.

'I wonder how long it will take for

her to phone someone to let us out?' Eve asked.

'Once she's off the island and safe, I presume. She's probably got more fake passports.'

'I left a note for Robert saying I was going to Joanna's, but he and his girlfriend might not come home till very late.'

'We'd better settle down and try to get some sleep. It'll make the time go faster.'

Eve nodded, but even though she sounded confident that they would be rescued, she was far from it. They weren't in either of Joanna's houses so how was anybody going to find them unless Joanna contacted the police?

19

Robert and Alison were having a lovely evening. They had been to Bella Sophia for a meal, and after filling themselves with garlic bread, mozzarella balls, avocado and Gorgonzola salad, not to mention sharing a large pizza, accompanied by an ice cold bottle of Frascati, they thought they would walk home and leave the car to be picked up in the morning.

However, as they walked back, they were sidetracked by the sound of live jazz coming from one of the bars. They both loved jazz and there was nothing for it, they had to go in and listen. Three drinks later, the music was still playing, but Alison was feeling decidedly tipsy and Robert insisted they went home. Greek measures were so much larger than English ones.

Once home, Alison and Robert went straight to bed without even bothering to have a glass of water. If they had gone into the kitchen, they might have seen the note which Eve had stuck on the fridge door and the search for Eve and Kevin might have begun a lot earlier.

* * *

Alison woke up at about six thirty the following morning. They hadn't got to bed until after two and she still felt shattered. However, she had a raging thirst.

No more of those gin and tonics for me. I'm sure they had more gin in them than tonic, she thought to herself.

Alison got up quietly so as not to disturb Robert. She found her dressing gown and went downstairs. Portia greeted her happily, indicating that she wanted to go out. Alison opened the back door and let Portia into the garden and then went to the fridge to get a glass of water. She still felt very groggy after drinking it and got another glass to take upstairs with her. As she shut the fridge door, she noticed a post-it note stuck onto it.

Where did that come from? she asked herself as she took the note off the door.

As she read it, she woke up immediately.

'When did Eve leave this? She can't have gone to Joanna's this early in the morning, can she?' she said aloud.

Alison dashed to the front door to see if Eve's car was parked outside. She vaguely remembered that the Mercedes hadn't been on the driveway when they had got home at two, but sometimes Eve would leave it on the road.

Running to the gate, Alison looked up and down the street. She was relieved when she saw Eve's Mercedes parked a few yards away, so she went back inside and up the stairs. However, the thought then crossed her mind that perhaps Eve had been drinking and might have walked to Joanna's. It would do no harm to check and Alison tiptoed to Eve's bedroom.

She hesitated for a moment, thinking that Eve wouldn't be too happy if she was woken up so early. However, it was important that she checked, so she knocked and opened the door a moment later. Alison was shocked to see that the bed hadn't been slept in and dashing back to her room, she started shaking Robert.

'What's going on?' he asked drowsily.

Alison quickly told him what had happened.

'And Eve isn't here, but her car is?' Robert asked anxiously. 'Perhaps we should try ringing her mobile.'

Robert got out of bed and found his phone. When he rang Eve, all he got was a voice telling him that the phone was switched off.

'Perhaps something had happened to David and she asked Annie to take her to the hospital,' he suggested. 'She hasn't been driving so well recently.

She's completely exhausted.'

'Why wouldn't she ask one of us to drive her?' Alison asked.

'Possibly because she heard us come home in the early hours.'

'I still think she would have told us, Robert.'

'Yes, you're probably right. It's also unusual for her to have her phone switched off.'

'I agree. I think we should go to Joanna's house now.'

* * *

Both Alison and Robert were annoyed that they had left their hire car close to Bella Sophia the previous evening, feeling that they were wasting time walking to collect it. However, it wasn't too far and soon they were driving towards Joanna's. As they approached her house, Alison spoke.

'Well, it looks like Joanna's in. There's a car in the driveway.'

'I wonder if Eve's in there as well?'

'I just hope Joanna hasn't done something stupid. If only we'd seen the note earlier.'

Oh God, what if we find Eve dead, Robert thought. *Why didn't we go into the kitchen last night? We would have found the note and been here much sooner . . .*

They both got out of the car quickly and Alison dashed ahead to ring the doorbell, but after ringing a few times, there was no reply.

'I think we should call the police,' Robert said. 'It would be silly if we broke in, don't you think?'

'I don't know,' answered Alison, who wasn't too sure if they should wait much longer.

'Eve gave me that officer's phone number, what's his name, Demitris Kastrinakis? I'll ring him direct.'

Dimitris was not too happy to be woken up so early, but once he was informed about what had happened, he told Robert to stay put and he would be there as soon as he could.

The next fifteen minutes were excruciating. Alison and Robert wandered around to the back of the house where they found a window with an open shutter. They peered in and saw that it was the kitchen. However, there was no sign of life. They tried the back door, but it wouldn't open. Both knew it was more sensible to wait for the police, but they were very restless.

'I've let her down,' Robert said dismally. 'I came to help her, but instead we were out till the early hours of the morning enjoying ourselves.'

'Don't blame yourself, Robert, you weren't to know that Eve would do this.'

'No, but I should have been prepared for her doing something wild and stupid. You know Eve, she's reckless and won't sit still.'

As Robert finished his sentence, Dimitris rolled up in his police car, with Stavros, who he had picked up on the way.

'When will that woman stop interfering in my investigations,' Dimitris said as soon as he met Alison and Robert.

'Don't speak like that about her,' Alison retorted. 'She's our friend and something is obviously very wrong. She could be in serious danger . . . or even worse.'

Alison's voice trailed off as she thought of the most horrible scenario.

'I'm sorry,' Dimitris replied. 'I too am concerned. I have become quite fond of Miss Masters, but she will keep doing these thoughtless and irresponsible things.'

Alison and Robert said nothing, knowing that Dimitris was right.

Dimitris and Stavros banged at the door and when there was no reply, they wandered around the outside of the house, Alison and Robert following a few steps behind. Seeing that the shutters of the kitchen window were open, Dimitris broke the pane of glass and told Stavros to climb in and let them in through the back door.

'Now, you two, stay in the kitchen while we search the house,' Dimitris instructed as soon as they were all inside.

Robert wanted to help in the search, but thought it best to let the police get on with their job. After all, they did have guns so they could better protect themselves.

The two police officers searched the house, including the basement, but came back to the kitchen shortly afterwards with news that there was no sign of anyone.

'It's very interesting that Joanna's car is still here,' Dimitris said. 'Perhaps she has left in the car of her accomplice. Possibly they have both taken Eve somewhere, but where?'

'Well,' Alison said, having just realised what they all seemed to have forgotten, 'nobody knows where they took David, do they? I reckon they've taken Eve to the same place.'

'Ah yes,' Dimitris replied. 'Of course, that would be very likely. If only Mr

Baker had remembered where it was.'

'Well he didn't,' Robert snapped, feeling that every minute was precious and they were wasting time talking when they should be looking for Eve.

Dimitris decided to disregard Robert's tone, knowing that both he and Alison were very upset about their friend's disappearance.

'Now we will go to the other house Joanna owns, but I have a feeling we'll find nobody there either,' Dimitris admitted.

Alison and Robert followed the police car, but again they were disappointed.

'What now?' Robert asked despondently.

'I have already circulated a description of Joanna Neonakis to the ports and airports, but I expect she has long gone.'

'What about Eve?' Alison asked.

'We will start a search, but I don't hold out much hope. Even if Eve is still alive, I fear Joanna would have hidden her well. I think we all have to prepare ourselves for the worst.'

20

David woke up early that same morning. His breathing was a little better than the previous day, but he felt nauseous again. He was feeling thoroughly fed up of being sick and wished more than anything that the effects of the poison would wear off.

A few minutes later, he started thinking about the nurse or whoever she was, coming in and giving him the injection. He had barely looked at her face, but he kept trying to visualise her.

It's no good, he thought a few minutes later. *I can't think what she looked like. And why can't I remember any more about the kidnapping? However, I'm beginning to think Eve is right and the person behind everything is Joanna.*

He couldn't imagine any of their close friends on the island going to such lengths to obtain money from Eve and he certainly didn't think any of them would try to kill him.

Of course you never really know people. He still found it hard to believe that Phyllis Baldwin could have been a murderer, or for that matter, Paul.

David was looking forward to seeing Eve that morning. He knew she would cheer him up. He had started brooding and having anxiety attacks, which wasn't like him. Thinking about his own mortality had taken up a large amount of his time while lying in that hospital bed.

He didn't know how Eve had managed to put all her brushes with death to the back of her mind. David didn't think he would ever get over this terrible experience. Instead he imagined spending the rest of his life having nightmares.

* * *

Eve and Kevin had also woken up early. Eve wanted to go to the bathroom, but didn't think she would be able to get there with her feet tied up so tightly.

'Well, I want to go to the loo as well,' Kevin said. 'And I'm hungry and I'm dying for a cup of black coffee.'

Eve wished he'd stop whinging.

'I'm sure it won't be long, Kevin,' Eve said, trying to sound optimistic. 'Joanna will probably ring someone to let us out as soon as she's off Greek soil.'

'How do you know, Eve? She's already shown she's a hard woman and it wouldn't surprise me if she didn't phone anybody and we rot to death in here.'

'Perhaps we should try and escape then.'

'And how are we going to do that? We're well and truly tied up and even if we get ourselves untied, how are we going to open the door. I heard her closing a bolt as well as a lock, so it'll be practically impossible.'

'Goodness, Kevin, you are negative, aren't you?' Eve said in exasperation.

He just shrugged his shoulders which annoyed Eve all the more.

'Why on earth did you get involved with Joanna, Kevin?' Eve asked the question that had been bothering her all night. 'It was so soon after Lucy's death.'

'Oh, so you're going to start criticising me, you who keeps getting into situations like this.'

'And I've always got out of them,' Eve jumped in quickly, annoyed by his comment. 'Anyway, you haven't told me why you went out with Joanna.'

'You've seen her, Eve, she's beautiful and young, and I thought she was keen on me. Anyway, Lucy and I were heading towards divorce.'

'Didn't you think it strange that Joanna took up with you so soon after Yiannis was murdered? I know she's just told us about her relationship with him, but you weren't to know the story. It would have been more likely that she would have been in love with Yiannis as they'd only just got married a few months previously. Didn't it ring any alarm bells?'

Kevin shrugged his shoulders again. He knew Eve was right, but he didn't want to admit it.

Eve's always right, he thought miserably. *What on earth did Joanna want with me? I really can't make it out. Was she just after my money, not that it amounts to a fortune?*

'I'm also surprised that she didn't rope you into the kidnapping, Kevin. Why did she choose someone else?'

'I don't know,' he snapped. 'Perhaps you should have asked her. I can't believe that I'm going to spend my last hours with you, I really can't.' He looked away.

Eve didn't bother to reply. He was also the last person she would wish to spend her last moments with. They had to try to escape.

'Why don't I try to untie your feet, Kevin? It will be difficult with my hands tied behind my back, but it's worth a go.'

Once in position, Eve began to try and loosen the rope around Kevin's feet with her hands still tied up. However, it was near on impossible. When Eve admitted defeat, Kevin tried to undo Eve's knots, but he too struggled. In the end, Eve had to admit that they were at Joanna's mercy.

* * *

After the police started their search for Eve, Robert and Alison felt at a loss. They didn't have any idea what they should do next.

'Robert,' Alison spoke at last. 'Do you think we should go and tell David?'

'I don't know. I've been thinking the same thing, but he's sick and I don't know if we should worry him. It might put back his recovery.'

'But he'll probably be expecting Eve to come and visit him. When she doesn't turn up, he'll be wondering where she is and will try to call her.'

Robert agreed that it might be best

after all if they did go to the hospital, but he wasn't looking forward to telling David the news about Eve.

* * *

David sat in stunned silence, with Alison and Robert standing by the side of his bed. He was trying to take it in, but it was difficult to comprehend that Eve was missing. How could she have been so reckless again? However, he didn't feel he could be cross with her this time. He knew he would have done the same if the roles were reversed.

'I'm so sorry that we had to bring you such bad news, David,' Alison said, taking his hand. 'However, we thought you should know.'

'I would have worried anyway when she didn't turn up this morning, so I had to know. I can't believe she was right though. She suspected Joanna all along.'

'It's a pity you didn't remember who

her accomplice was, David,' Robert put in. 'Mind you, it does look like it could be Kevin.'

'I've been wracking my brains since I've been here and it just won't come to me. I find it really hard to believe that her accomplice is Kevin though. Kevin and I have become good friends recently.' He shook his head sadly.

'I'm sorry,' Alison said. 'Of course, it might not be him.'

An awkward silence followed.

'They might have put Eve in the house where they put me,' he said, forgetting about Kevin for the time being. 'I just can't remember where it was. Damn, I feel useless.'

'Try and get some rest,' Alison said. 'I know it's hard, but it might help you remember.'

David nodded, but he didn't know how he would be able to sleep with Eve missing.

* * *

The police had started their search, but Dimitris wasn't holding out much hope. There was a large area to cover and it would take a lot of manpower, manpower which they didn't have.

If they came across any new houses which were partially built, they decided to search them. There was a possibility that Eve could have been locked up in one of them.

'This is impossible,' Stavros said to his boss.

'We have to keep looking,' Dimitris replied.

Suddenly he thought of something.

'Joanna was often seen with Kevin Fowler. We're going to his house next.'

It wasn't far from where they were so it took just five minutes to get there.

Reaching the house, Dimitris knocked at the door a couple of times, but there was no reply. He also noticed that there wasn't a car parked in the driveway.

'I don't like this,' Dimitris remarked. 'Perhaps he's gone off with Joanna Neonakis. We'll get a search warrant for his house. You never know, Eve could be locked up in there.'

* * *

David was surprised that he had been able to sleep, despite his concern for Eve. He had been through a great deal and hadn't had a proper night's sleep since before he was kidnapped.

As David sat up, he suddenly realised that he could remember more about what had happened in the past few days.

'I remember who he was, the man that kidnapped me,' he said out loud.

Astonished by this turn of events, he grabbed his mobile and phoned Dimitris Kastrinakis. Dimitris had given him his direct number in case he recalled anything about his ordeal.

'Nai,' Dimitris said as usual. He never seemed to have the time to be polite.

'Inspector Kastrinakis, this is David Baker. I've remembered who my kidnapper was. It was Wayne, Wayne Fowler.'

* * *

Dimitris and Stavros took another two officers with them and drove to Wayne Fowler's house. Dimitris knew exactly where it was as it was Paul Fowler's home. Wayne was staying there and looking after it for Paul.

Arriving there, Dimitris told two of the officers to go round to the back of the house in case Wayne tried to make a run for it. His car was outside the house so they imagined that Wayne was in.

Dimitris rang the doorbell, but there was no answer. Wayne was, in fact, still in bed. He turned over, hoping that whoever it was would go away. His body was aching from where David had hit him. Dimitris rang the doorbell again and started banging at the door. Reluctantly Wayne got up and looked out of the window. He almost passed out when he saw the police activity.

He hurriedly went and put on a pair of trousers and a T-shirt and quietly went downstairs, planning to escape out the back, but as he opened the door, the officers grabbed him and pushed him back inside. They led him to the front door and one of them opened it. Wayne was confronted by Dimitris and Stavros.

'What's going on?' he asked, trying to maintain an air of innocence.

'There's no point pretending you have no idea why we're here, Mr Fowler. David has identified you as his kidnapper and we have come to arrest you,' Dimitris announced.

Wayne was silent. He had no idea what to do now. He could deny it, but they wouldn't believe him. It was all over.

'We would like you to take us to where you kept David.'

'Why?'

'We have reason to believe that Joanna Neonakis has put Eve Masters there, too,' Dimitris answered.

'Why don't you ask Joanna?' Wayne continued. He didn't feel like being helpful. He was going to jail whatever happened.

'Mrs Neonakis has disappeared. We think she has already left the island, possibly the country.'

Wayne said nothing, but he was fuming inside.

She's left me to take the blame for everything, he thought, his anger rising.

'It'll help you in the long run if you help us now,' Dimitris added.

Wayne didn't know if that would turn out to be the case, but he didn't want anyone else hurt. That wasn't the plan and if Joanna had locked Eve up in that basement, there was no way of getting out.

'OK, I'll take you there,' Wayne finally agreed.

* * *

Ten minutes later the police and Wayne arrived at an estate of half finished houses and Wayne directed them to one house in particular.

Entering the house, Wayne took them to the basement door. There was a lock and a large bolt across it. Luckily the key was still in the lock. Dimitris ordered Wayne to open the door and once he had done so, Dimitris called down. He immediately got an answer.

'We're down here, tied up,' Eve shouted.

Dimitris, Stavros, Wayne and the other two officers trooped downstairs and as soon as Wayne reached the basement floor, he gasped.

'Dad, what are you doing here?'

'I could ask you the same question, son,' Kevin replied, sounding bemused.

'Your son, Mr Fowler, is under arrest,' Dimitris said immediately. 'He is one of the kidnappers, the other being Joanna Neonakis, as you no doubt know.'

'Wayne, how could you do such a thing? And with Joanna . . . '

'She promised that once we'd got the

money, we'd be together.'

'But what about your wife and the kids, son?'

'I'm so sorry, Dad. I was swept away by her.'

'But you knew she was seeing me.'

'She said it was just a cover because I was married and she wanted us to be a secret.'

Kevin shook his head and Eve thought he looked devastated. He really must have been keen on that awful woman. She decided that they needed to change the subject.

'I don't know about Kevin, but I would appreciate being untied. I'm desperate for the bathroom as well as aching all over.'

'Yes, untie them please,' Dimitris shouted to his officers.

'Did you manage to catch Joanna?' Eve asked Dimitris as she was being untied.

'I'm afraid not. It's highly likely that she's changed identities again.'

'That's unfortunate, but hopefully

she's gone far away and doesn't grace Greece with her presence again.'

'But I'll have to take the punishment for everything now,' Wayne moaned.

'You will only be blamed for your part, Mr Fowler,' Dimitris said. 'However, kidnapping is a major crime and you won't get off lightly.'

Good, Eve thought. *He deserves everything coming his way after what he did to my David. It's a pity they didn't catch Joanna, but I doubt if we'll ever see her again, thank goodness*.

* * *

In a first class seat on a plane from Athens to Perth, Australia, a very attractive woman with blonde hair sat drinking champagne. She was leaning back to relax when the flight attendant came over.

'Another glass of champagne?'

'I shouldn't, but why not? One more won't hurt. Thank you.'

'Have you decided what you'd like

for lunch, Mrs Castle?' the flight attendant then asked.

'Yes, thank you. Scallops, followed by steak, medium rare.'

Ah, this is the life, she thought. *Australia here I come*.

21

All Eve wanted to do was to see David, but the police were asking so many questions. Then she had to go home to have a bath and get a change of clothes after such an unpleasant night in that dusty basement.

Dimitris was worried about her driving to the hospital after having had so little sleep, but she said that Robert would take her.

It was almost midday when Eve finally arrived at the hospital.

Robert and Alison went to see Betty and Pete so that Eve could have a few private moments with David.

Dashing into his ward, she threw her arms around him and kissed him firmly on the lips, not caring if she planted all her lipstick there.

'Wow, that was some greeting,' David said, hugging her close.

'Oh, darling. Last night was so awful that I did occasionally doubt if I would ever see you again.'

'Oh Eve, don't say that. I've been out of my mind with worry too. I'm so sorry I didn't believe you about Joanna until nearly the end. I don't know why I didn't. You've been right so many times before.'

'Don't worry about it,' Eve replied, for once being humble.

'So,' David asked, 'I've been told there was something going on romantically between Joanna and Wayne. Is it true?'

'Sort of,' Eve said. 'But it was all promises, similar to what she promised Kevin. I do feel sorry for Kevin, even though he was a pain last night. He complained all the time. But not only was he tied up by the woman he loved, but he also had to discover that his son's a bad lot.'

David took Eve's hands in his.

'Thank goodness it's over, darling,' he said, looking into her eyes. 'These past few hours have been terrible; thinking I might lose you.'

'It was the same for me when you'd been kidnapped,' she admitted, holding back the tears that were threatening to spill over.

Eve bent down and kissed David gently, her stomach doing somersaults as if it was the first time their lips had touched.

Suddenly they heard a cough behind them and they separated. Eve looked round and saw Annie and Pete.

'Hello, you two,' Eve said. 'Glad to see you up and about, Pete.'

'Yes, off home now,' he replied. 'We feel as if a weight's been lifted off our shoulders now the real kidnappers have been identified. Hope you'll be out of here soon as well, David.'

'Me too, I've had enough of this hospital to last me a lifetime.'

'I think we all have,' Eve commented, while the others all grinned.

* * *

A couple of days later, David was also released from hospital. Eve was delighted that he was coming back home.

The phone rang as soon as they stepped into the hallway and while Eve answered it, David went and sat in the lounge.

He still didn't feel as if he had much energy, but he knew it would probably take him time to get back to his former self.

A few minutes later, Eve came bounding in, looking excited.

'What's up, darling?' David asked. He was intrigued by her change of mood.

'The phone call was from a lawyer in Australia telling me my second cousin, Andrea, has died and left me something in her will. We have to go to Australia to collect it; Perth I believe. Won't that be amazing?'

'Aren't you upset about your cousin,' David asked, surprised by her manner.

'Oh, Andrea and I haven't seen each

other since we were about five. We barely knew each other even then,' she admitted.

David nodded. He didn't want to argue with Eve, not on his first day out of hospital. Anyway, the idea of a trip to Australia sounded like fun, especially after all they'd both been through.

'So, when do we leave for Australia?' he asked instead, looking bemused.

'In about a week's time. So, you're keen to go?' Eve asked, trying for once to take his opinion into account.

'Yes, very much. I think it'll do us both good to get away from Crete for a while.'

* * *

That evening, David and Eve walked into The Black Cat. David still felt a little tired and weak, but he wanted to go to the bar for Jane's leaving do. She was going back to England the following day, having changed her flight so that David would be able to attend her party.

Pete and Annie were there, as well as Kevin. Kevin hadn't wanted to come, but Eve had persuaded him, saying it would do him good and might take his mind off Wayne and Joanna.

Robert and Alison were also guests, both going back to England in a couple of days' time.

Betty was still in hospital, while Don, who was still adamant that he wasn't giving up on their divorce, had also come to wish Jane a fond farewell. He was going to miss her.

Half way through the evening, Eve decided it was time to make a speech, so she went and ordered everyone drinks on her and then she stood up.

'Well, I'd just like to say a few words. The last week or so has been very difficult; not only for myself and David, but for others in this room, in particular, our good friend, Pete, who the police suspected to be David's kidnapper. All this has made me realise how many good friends we have here and one of these has been Jane. We're going to miss you very much and we're looking forward to seeing you next year for the wedding, if not sooner. The same goes for you, Robert and Alison. Thank you both for coming over — I'm sure Betty would be thanking you, Alison, if she were here. David and I will be going away next week to Australia for a well earned rest, so you'll have to do without us for a few weeks. Anyway, that's all I have to say for the present. Let's just enjoy the evening and a big thank you to Ken and Jan for the lovely spread.'

Everybody clapped and Eve sat down looking pleased with herself.

'Well done, my darling,' David whispered, taking her hand. He knew how much Eve loved being the centre of attention.

Eve squeezed David's hand and smiled, visions of herself in her beautiful wedding dress floating through her mind.

Oh yes, it was going to be a perfectly

wonderful day when the stunning Eve Masters married her soul mate, David Baker the following summer. To hell with murders and kidnappings. She'd had enough to last her a lifetime. All she wanted now was David. She had realised that when she thought she was going to lose him.

They were going to have a wonderful time together in Australia where they would be able to grow even closer.

Eve pulled David nearer and put her arm through his before kissing him. When their lips parted, David smiled at Eve and stroked her hand.

I think Eve is finally happy with her life here and with me, he thought. *I doubt if she'll need the excitement of murders and mysteries to keep her occupied after what's just happened. We have a fantastic trip planned which will herald a brand new start for us. I can't wait to see what the future holds for us.*

Other titles in the
Linford Romance Library:

FAR FROM HOME

Jean Robinson

At 23, Dani has an exciting chance at a new life when her mother Francine invites her to live with her in Paris and join her fashion business. What's more, Dani has fallen in love with Claude, Francine's right-hand man. But it's anything but plain sailing at home in England, where Dani has been living with her father, who is on the edge of a breakdown from stress and doesn't want her to leave. What will Dani choose to do — and is Claude willing to wait while she decides?

LEAVING LISA

Angela Britnell

At age seventeen, married with a three-month-old baby and suffering from post-natal depression, all Rosie could see was her life in a cage with a giant lock. Twenty-five years later, after having left her husband Jack and daughter Lisa, she runs her own business in Nashville. But while she's in England, she sees an engagement announcement in the newspaper — Lisa is getting married. And Rosie decides she wants to make contact after all these years, despite fearing their reaction. Will they find room in their hearts for her again?

RUNNING FROM DANGER

Sarah Purdue

Pregnant and alone, Rebecca flees to the US in a bid to escape her ex and his ties to organised crime. There she meets Sheriff Will Hayes in a small backwater town — but can she trust him? When she tries to make a run for it, Will stops her and suggests a plan that involves them both. But Rebecca is unsure of his feelings for her. Can Will keep her safe from her ex and his crime-boss father? Or will the biggest risk come from falling in love?

COOKING UP A STORM

Judy Jarvie

Artist and entrepreneur Amy Chambers runs a quirky but popular café and art studio in Derbyshire with her sister Lorna. When they win the chance to be mentored by a celebrated business angel who will assist with their expansion, it's an exciting prospect — until Amy realises it will put her head to head with the country's most renowned celebrity chef and global gourmet, Mal Donaldson, who takes no prisoners. Can Mal find a way to convince her that together they have the perfect ingredients for lasting happiness?

THE EIGHTH CHILD

Margaret Mounsdon

Why is Posy Palmer the only one to be concerned when her old school friend, Iris Laxton, disappears? But as Posy begins to delve into Iris's past, she realises how little she really knew about her. When Posy's bicycle tyre is deliberately punctured, and evidence begins to disappear, the only person she can turn to for help is Sam Barrington, the charismatic ex-policeman who accused her of wasting police time when she reported another missing person six months previously. Will he believe her this time?

THE GOLDEN BUTTERFLY

Jane Lester

When Eileen Amberley's longtime friend Richard takes up a position as a doctor at Vickersands Hospital, she goes there herself, to train as a nurse and hope their relationship will lead to marriage. Instead, she finds herself watching the dazzling Heather Maple capture Richard's affections, and is heartbroken. Then she meets the attractive, enigmatic Jeff Watt, who works on the waterfront — and keeps a secret. By the time Eileen discovers the truth, is it too late for the two of them to acknowledge their feelings and make a life together?